TENDER IS THE TOUCH

Anne Shore

For Fleur, it was just the big break she needed. Fresh out of design school, she'd landed a dream assignment. For one month she'd study Mayan ruins in the exotic Yucatán, then she'd be off to her first showing of original fashions.

But here in Mexico, she must work and survive . . . survive the mysterious intrigue of her colleagues . . . and survive the changeable moods of Matt Kirkpatrick, his burning looks, his icy indifference . . . survive the shiver of joy she felt at the sight of his long, lean body – but could she survive his warm and gentle kiss . . . ?

ANNE SHORE

TENDER IS THE TOUCH

Curley Publishing, Inc.
South Yarmouth, Ma.

Library of Congress Cataloging-in-Publication Data

Shore, Anne.
  Tender is the touch / Anne Shore.
    p. cm.
  1. Large type books. I. Title.
[PS3569.H5792T4 1989]
813'.54—dc19
ISBN 1–55504–929–X (lg. print)   89–623
ISBN 1–55504–911–7 (pbk. : lg. print)   CIP

Published in Large Print by arrangement with Donald MacCampbell, Inc. in the United States, Canada, the U.K. and British Commonwealth.

Distributed in Great Britain, Ireland and the Commonwealth by CHIVERS LIBRARY SERVICES LIMITED, Bath BA1 3HB, England.

Printed in Great Britain

TENDER IS THE TOUCH

Chapter One

"The Yucatán!" Fleur Normandy flashed a dazzling smile at her companion behind the wheel of the jeep in which the two of them were riding down the flat, rather monotonous highway to Chichén Itzá. "I can't believe I'm actually here."

"You'll believe it," Eric Spandell answered with a cynical smile. "When the first *garrapata* sinks his pincers into you."

"Garra-what?" Fleurs gray eyes widened beneath the canvas cap pulled far down on her brow to control the wind-whipped masses of her lustrous black hair. "What on earth is that?"

"Cattle ticks. So elusive you aren't aware of them until you're covered." The cynical smile appeared again. "Of course by that time, it's too late."

Fleur pulled up one leg of her jeans and peered anxiously at a trim ankle. "Isn't there anything one can do?"

"Here." Spandell reached into a canvas bag on the seat between them and pulled out

1

a can of insect repellent. "Spray thoroughly with that."

Fleur doused her ankles and the legs of her jeans. "Enough?"

Spandell nodded.

"Good you brought that along," she said with a grateful smile.

"I didn't do so by accident, I can assure you. I learned the hard way."

"Oh. Then you've been to the Yucatán before?"

"Summer, a year ago," he answered. "I came down to Cancun to work up some resort brochures, and I wandered around a bit."

Fleur gazed across at the slight man of about her own age seated behind the wheel. Beneath a thatch of ash blond hair and a wide forehead burned a pair of small, penetrating brown eyes – capable, she suspected, of assimilating minute details with no more than a cursory glance. Not a bad attribute for a professional photographer, she acceded, but rather discomfiting to one like herself making his acquaintance for the first time.

An hour ago he had met her with the jeep when her New York flight arrived at the Mérida Airport, and now they were headed toward a hacienda near Chichén Itzá where they would join the other member of their team, Rita Pittman, a young Philadelphia archaeologist with whom they would be working for the next month.

"Is this your jeep?" Fleur looked around at her hurriedly assembled possessions crowded in among Spandell's suitcases and photographic equipment.

Spandell shook his head. "Kirkpatrick's. One of his colleagues drove it to Mérida from the hacienda yesterday. I was coming in on a flight just as he was leaving, so it worked out handily."

"Except that you had to lay over a day waiting for me," Fleur smiled. "I appreciate that."

Spandell shrugged. "I had no choice."

Fleur stared, taken aback by this blunt answer. Certainly no one could accuse Eric Spandell of flattery! Still, he had seemed pleasant enough up to now, and they did have to work together for the next few months. There was nothing to be gained by taking offense.

"You're acquainted with Rita Pittman, I believe you said, but do you know Dr. Kirkpatrick?" Fleur's curiosity had been piqued a number of times during her flight by thoughts of their host, a well-known archaeologist currently associated with the National Museum in Mexico City.

"Only by reputation," Spandell eyed her languidly. "I understand he's a real devil with women."

Fleur, who had expected a professional assessment, not a personal exposé, flushed.

"He's in his mid-thirties, I understand. Rich. Single." Spandell's lip curled. "And, according to the ladies, quite handsome."

"How nice for him," said Fleur coolly.

Spandell laughed. "You're not interested?"

"I came down here to work," Fleur answered crisply. Then breathing deeply of the clear November air, she said with a sigh. "And I think this is a heavenly place to do it."

A smirk twisted Spandell's sensitive mouth. "We'll see how long that impression lasts."

Annoyed, Fleur turned to face him. "Why shouldn't it last? An incredible stroke of good fortune had made possible this opportunity, and she was not about to let this man's jaded views spoil her excitement.

The smirk deepened. "You've never worked with Rita Pittman, have you?"

"I've never worked with anyone. I've only just finished at The School of Design in New York."

4

"My. Then you've landed quite a plum – for a newcomer."

"I'd say having a part in a Flaxendon opening is quite a plum for anyone, newcomer or not." Her spirited answer brought a grudging nod from Spandell.

"Barry Flaxendon does make quite a splash in moneyed circles," he agreed. "And the Mayan exhibition will have just enough pizzazz to pull in the big fish from all over the East."

The exhibition Spandell referred to was scheduled to open in April at the privately endowed Flaxendon Museum in Philadelphia. Barry Flaxendon, its young benefactor, had in mind featuring a collection of rare Yucatecan artifacts and at the same time introducing a matching line of Mayan designer clothes and jewelry, which, conveniently enough, would be distributed only by his exclusive clothing store, Flaxendon & Company.

Rita Pittman had been chosen to coordinate the archaeological background for the exhibit, Spandell to do the photography, and Fleur – though she was still dazed by the fabulous opportunity – had been assigned to work up the designs for the clothing and jewelry. Following a month's study of the Mayan ruins and the surrounding area,

5

the three of them were to adjourn to Philadelphia replete with fresh ideas, stacks of photographs and background information, and sketches for a designer line Flaxendon anticipated would knock the eyes out of the New York establishment.

Fleur felt the spasm of nervous anticipation that clutched her each time she thought of the heavy responsibility she had accepted when Barry Flaxendon had approached her with the job offer less than a week before. "We all have our special fields," she said now to Spandell, "but our total success hinges on Dr. Kirkpatrick, I suppose."

Spandell grimaced. "I hope not!"

Fleur regarded him with surprise. "Kirkpatrick *is* the world's leading authority on the Mayan ruins, isn't he?"

"No question about that," Spandell's laugh was brittle. "But it doesn't necessarily follow he's going to share his expertise with us."

"But why else would he invite us to spend a month in his house?"

"Point number one: only half of the house is his. Point number two: he didn't invite us. Faxendon did."

"But surely with Dr. Kirkpatrick's permission!"

"Flaxendon didn't need permission," replied Spandell in a bored tone. "He's the owner of the other half of the hacienda. He can ask whom he pleases."

Fleur digested this unexpected bit of news. "Do you mind explaining how such an unwieldy arrangement came about?"

"Gladly," said Spandell with the sardonic grin she was coming to know so well. "They're stepbrothers. Two years ago Flaxendon's mother, who was living at Cozumel, swept old man Kirkpatrick off his feet. He died shortly after they were married, but not before he changed his will, leaving her the lion's share of the estate. Unfortunately, she didn't live to enjoy it. She died in a plane crash a month later off the Isle of Mujeres. Flaxendon is the sole heir to her portion. He and Matt Kirkpatrick have been battling it out in the courts ever since. They hate each other."

"I see," murmured Fleur. "That leaves us all in a rather uncomfortable situation, doesn't it?"

"To say the least!"

"Maybe he won't even be there," Fleur said hopefully, picturing the reputedly handsome face of Dr. Kirkpatrick glowering with fury.

"Oh, he's there all right. The colleague

7

who handed over the jeep said he's digging his heels in."

Fleur stared in alarm. "But he can't forbid us use of the house, can he?"

"I doubt it, but he could make things so unpleasant, we might abandon it of our own accord. He has terrific influence in archaeological circles too, don't forget. A lot of doors could be closed to us if he gave the word." Spandell's mask of superiority had slipped a little, and to her surprise, Fleur found the waning of his assurance at this point even more disconcerting than his arrogance. "Poor Rita! I wonder how she's faring."

Spandell snorted. "Don't waste your pity. If anybody can whip Kirkpatrick into shape, it's Pittman."

Well, Fleur thought, at least Spandell had confidence in *someone*. "Didn't the fellow with the jeep give any indication of how things were going?"

Eric shook his head. "Only that he predicted we'd probably last about a week. Two at the most."

They rode in silence for a while, each one staring glumly ahead at the flat terrain of the peninsula. Finally Fleur turned a brighter face toward Spandell.

"I think we're forgetting one very

important point. Even if Dr. Kirkpatrick does despise his stepbrother, the man is still an archaeologist. He's bound to be pleased that the Mayan artifacts are to have such a splendid display. Perhaps that alone will insure his cooperation."

Spandell shot her a pitying glance. "The artifacts are the biggest bone of contention between Flaxendon and Kirkpatrick. If Kirkpatrick had inherited them as he certainly expected to, he planned to give them to the National Museum. The fact that Flaxendon got them and carted them out of the country galls him more than anything."

"I don't understand," said Fleur, frowning. "How could anyone expect to inherit artifacts? Shouldn't they have belonged to the government in the first place, rather than to an individual?"

"If they were discovered today, national interests most certainly would control them," replied Spandell. "But years ago the government had more pressing things to do with their money than to use it digging in pyramids and vacuuming sacrificial wells. Old man Kirkpatrick financed the explorations, and he kept the spoils."

"But that doesn't seem fair to the cultural heritage of the country!"

"That's what Matt Kirkpatrick thinks,
9

too, and if he'd gotten the chance, he would have made amends by returning them to Mexico."

Score one for Matt Kirkpatrick, thought Fleur, not quite sure where, in her categorized version of Kirkpatrick as the villain, this latest bit of information fit.

"But enough of gloom and doom," said Spandell in a lighter tone. "Just for the record, tell me how a novice like yourself managed to land such a juicy job – if indeed it turns out to be that."

Fleur had her own doubts about the outcome now, but still she could not suppress the excitement which the original offer to be a part of the Flaxendon project had generated. "I won a prize," she answered with a smile that lit her luminous gray eyes and lifted appealingly the corners of her ripe, red lips. "The Senior School of Design Medal of Distinction." Enthusiasm bubbled from Fleur, and even the cynical Eric Spandell could not resist it.

"Sounds like you really wowed them with something."

"I still don't know where such a fantastic idea came from. It just popped out of my head one morning at breakfast, and I raced off to the zoo."

"The zoo!"

10

She laughed. "I worked up a line of evening wear designs from the patterns in animal pelts."

Spandell frowned. "Fur designs?"

"No. No! The arrangements of the spots and stripes – that sort of thing. Then I laid them out surrealistically for fabric designs." Her eyes sparkled. "It was so much fun! I loved it, and fortunately so did the judges."

Spandell eyed her with a look of grudging admiration. "Then it was your imagination that hooked Flaxendon?"

Fleur nodded. "He was one of the judges. He said he wanted the freshest, newest talent he could find for his exhibition." Fleur laughed exuberantly. "Me! I hope I can come up with something to merit his confidence."

"Oh, you're young, pretty." The bitterness in Spandell's voice chilled Fleur. "You can go a long way on those two tickets."

In spite of the compliment Fleur bristled. "Well, if you think I intend to, you're badly mistaken."

Spandell shot her a superior look.

"Besides," she went on hotly. "I'm not all that young. It's taken me six years working full time as a secretary to get through design school. And believe me, no one there gave marks according to the tilt of an person's

11

nose or the length of her eyelashes!"

Spandell accepted the rebuke with a grin. "I'm glad to see you have spirit. Even if Kirkpatrick turns out to be a lamb, you'll need it with Rita Pittman."

"That's your second rather gloomy reference to Miss Pittman." Fleur gave him a challenging glance. "What is she? Some kind of two-headed ogre?"

Spandell gave a short laugh. "Hardly. But she knows what she wants. And she usually gets it."

"Good! If what you've heard about Matt Kirkpatrick is true, we'll need her kind of drive."

Spandell glanced across at the dark-haired girl who looked more like a fashion model than a designer and reflected that Rita Pittman would be far from happy to meet Fleur Normandy. "I hope you still feel that way tomorrow."

"I'm sure I shall." But Fleur's voice carried more conviction than she felt. To be skyrocketed to the heights on one's first venture was flattering, but it had a price. If one failed, one had just that much further to fall.

But why should she fall?

Her faltering confidence responded to logic. Even if Matt Kirkpatrick did dislike

12

her employer, their quarrel had nothing to do with her. Besides, the fact that she had been chosen for the job was no accident. There was special quality, a keenness, to her work, which set it apart. She was aware of this, but took no credit for it, accepting it gratefully as a talent to be nurtured and developed to its fullest potential, a process she found fascinating and absorbing. Whatever else went on around her at the Kirkpatrick hacienda, she would be doing the work she loved, and she knew that went a long way toward insuring success.

Furthermore, there was too much at stake for her not to succeed. Not only was her career on the line, but Barbara and her mother were depending on her. This was Barbara's first year in college and the first year as well in which her mother's arthritis prevented her from working as a seamstress. Even with Barb employed part time, there was no way expenses could be met without Fleur's help.

"According to my instructions, this should be our turnoff." Spandell slowed the jeep and swung sharply to the left where a wide, crushed stone road met the highway.

"So many trees!" said Fleur, who in her musings had failed to notice the miles of flat, green fields giving way to scrubby growth,

13

which in turn was rapidly developing into a forest. "I'd pictured a desert."

"Parts of the peninsula do fit that description," said Spandell, "but the rainfall is heavier throught this area, so there's some low jungle growth." He glanced at the encroaching greenery. "It's rather nice, isn't it."

Fleur nodded in agreement, once more breathing deeply of the crystal freshness in the air. "What's it like here in the summer?"

"Wet. Hot. October and November are the finest months. The light's perfect for the camera."

"For the paintbrush, too," murmured Fleur, wishing fervently she had one in her hand so that she might capture the atmosphere of the forest primeval that prevailed all about them. "What a glorious spot for a home. No wonder Matt Kirkpatrick is hanging on to his half."

"I'm beginning to wonder if we'll ever find the damned place," muttered Spandell, but then suddenly there it was: a low, rambling hacienda of dazzling white stucco set like a diamond in an oval clearing just ahead. Above it, coco palms waved lazily, and draping its spun sugar sides were crimson bougainvillea. A wide veranda stretched across the front, and to the left a crescent-shaped pool as blue as the sky above it in the center of a tile terrace where a man and woman sat together.

"Well, at least they're still on speaking terms," murmured Spandell, pulling the jeep to a stop at the end of a walkway a few feet from the pool.

"Rita?" Fleur tensed. "And is that Dr. Kirkpatrick with her?"

"I'd assume so." Spandell eyed the lean, muscular form of the dark-haired man rising slowly to greet them.

He was well over six feet, Fleur estimated as she climbed from the jeep. And younger than she had expected. He wore jeans and a coarse denim shirt open at the throat to reveal a mass of hair the same jet black as that which grew thickly on his head. His eyes were black too, and set deeply beneath heavy dark brows, but it was his mouth that captured Fleur's attention. The lips were firm, moderately full, and gently curved, though not in a smile. They were a witness to strength and assertiveness that drew Fleur like a magnet, and for one absurd moment she had to steel herself against a wrenching desire to taste them.

"I'm Fleur Normandy." She felt her hand enclosed firmly, her eyes locked in a

15

probing gaze that sent a shiver up her spine.

"Matt Kirkpatrick." The voice was low, coldly polite. "Have you met Miss Pittman?"

The woman by the pool had risen languidly, and as she strolled toward them, Fleur was aware at once of the pride the other woman took in her body. The jeans covering her narrow hips and legs were as tight as a second skin, and the tails of her white shirt were knotted beneath full, rounded breasts to expose a tanned midriff. Murky green eyes moved slowly up Fleur's body, rested briefly on her face, and flicked to Spandell. "Ah, *Eric.*" She gave the name a twist, making it almost a sneer.

Ignoring the greeting, Spandell set his bags down and extended his hand to Matt Kirkpatrick. "Eric Spandell. I'm an admirer of your work, sir."

"And I yours," Kirkpatrick responded with a brief smile. "I've seen your coal mining series in the Dublin Museum. My illustrious stepbrother did well to secure you for his –" a glint of steel flickered in the black eyes "– exhibition, I believe he calls it."

Rita Pittman's snub had disconcerted Fleur for a moment only, the other woman's rudeness taking second place immediately to the fascination Fleur found in observing

16

the change which had come over Spandell. The moment he stepped from the jeep an almost boyish eagerness replaced his sardonic attitude, and at Dr. Kirkpatrick's praise, he began to positively glow.

Rita, on the other hand, appeared enormously annoyed. "It's almost time for lunch. You two had better get settled in your rooms."

Fleur turned back toward the jeep, but Matt Kirkpatrick's low voice arrested her. "Ramon will bring your things in, and Josie's somewhere in the house. She'll show you where you'll be staying."

Fleur smiled her thanks and set off up the walk, followed by Rita and Eric. When they were out of Kirkpatrick's earshot, Rita murmured in a voice heavy with sarcasm, "Dear Spandell. How could I be so lucky as to get you twice running?"

Spandell's sharp retort came back like gunfire. "You haven't got me, Rita. You never did have." Behind her, Fleur heard his cynical laugh. "And if you've got any ideas about Kirkpatrick forget them. He's way out of your league."

Chapter Two

When Fleur opened the front door of the hacienda, she felt as if she had stepped from one world into another. The interior was cloistered and cool; spacious, yet cozily comfortable; open, yet private.

This paradoxical effect was achieved, she discovered after a moment, by the arrangement of the rooms around a central patio, visible at the end of the entryway and from each of the rooms surrounding the glassed-in enclosure. A fountain splashed at its middle, lush tropical plants sprang up in profusion, and birds sang in the tops of swaying palms.

"How absolutely charming!" Fleur turned breathlessly to survey the long, sunken living room to her left, the elegant dining room to her right with a sunny kitchen beyond, and an inviting array of rooms leading off in both directions from the entryway.

Spandell set down his bags and uttered a low whistle, "Where's the dividing line?"

Fleur giggled. "I was wondering the same thing!"

Rita scowled. "What?"

"Which part belongs to Flaxendon," said Eric, "and which to Kirkpatrick?"

"Oh, really!" Rita's expression was one of pure disgust. "I hope you two don't air your childish curiosity in front of Matt."

Eric smiled sardonically. "Matt, is it?"

Ignoring him, Rita went on. "He's very sensitive about his legal problems, and since he's been nice enough to offer us his hospitality in spite of them, it's certainly to our advantage not to mention the subject."

Fleur spoke eagerly. "Do you mean he's going to work with us?"

Rita turned a cold look in her direction. "I didn't say that. But providing no one gets out of line –" she leveled her gaze on Spandell "– he won't oppose us."

"You've seen to that, of course," said Spandell.

Rita's green eyes flashed. "You'd better be thankful I have! He wasn't at all happy about our coming here, and I've spent three days working him around to my point of view. I hope you have enough sense not to spoil it."

"*Your* point of view?" Spandell's brown eyes sparked. "Where does that leave Fleur and me?"

"We're all in this together," Rita snapped. "Though if I'd had my way —"

"Hold it right there!" Eric glared. "I got this job on my own merits, and so did Fleur. We're as qualified for it as you are. Let's have that understood from the start."

Fleur blinked in astonishment. After observing Spandell's lofty attitude on the ride out from Mérida, it was amazing to hear him now defending her as if she were a colleague. Which of course she was, she acknowledged with some surprise. And he was right to set things straight with Rita. Fleur took in Rita Pittman's set mouth and flashing eyes. She might be a highly qualified archaeologist, but she fell short of a pleasing personality by a country mile! Fleur felt a decided warming toward the slight, young photographer stolidly returning Rita's acid look, but there was a decided need for peacemaking.

"See here, you two." The lightness in Fleur's tone belied her nervousness. "The next four weeks here and the months afterward in Philadelphia are going to be much easier for all of us if we can manage to be pleasant. And I don't see why we can't. We're all here for the same thing: to make a success of the exhibition. So let's forget our differences and concentrate on that. Frankly,

I'm quite pleased that you've managed to convince Dr. Kirkpatrick that our cause is worthy." She smiled at Rita. "And since you have, I think we can look forward to a productive session." She smiled again. "And to lunch, I hope. I'm starved!"

As if she had overheard Fleur's remark, a fat, plain-faced woman with black hair wound around her head in tight braids emerged from the kitchen. "Josie," she said with a wide smile. "I show you rooms." She grinned toothily at Fleur. "Then I feed."

The men's bedrooms, Josie explained, were on the opposite side of the patio from Rita's and Fleur's, and Eric wandered off to the right with a set of hazy instructions while Fleur followed Josie and Rita toward the left until they came, three doors down, to a room painted a pale pink and carpeted in what appeared to be white fur.

"This is mine?" Fleur stepped gingerly onto the white cloud. The bed was covered by a soft, quilted spread, and a dressing room following the same pink-and-white color scheme opened beyond it. The wall opposite was glass and looked out onto the patio.

"My room is next door," said Rita. Then consulting her watch she said crisply, "Josie rings a triangle for lunch and dinner. When

21

you hear it, come at once. Matt despises stragglers."

"Will I have time for a shower?"

But Rita had already disappeared through the doorway. Shrugging, Fleur stepped into the dressing room and shut the door. Time or not, she had to get out of her clothes and into some warm water. She was grateful to Eric for saving her from the *garrapatas,* but the smell of the citronella repellent could very well alienate others besides the ticks!

In the bathroom, fluffy pink towels had been laid out and a bar of expensive soap perfumed the air daintily the moment it touched the water. For as long as she dared, Fleur luxuriated under the tingling spray, vigor returning to her tired body as fatigue slipped away.

Stepping out, she toweled dry, realizing as she did so that she had no clothes other than those she had traveled in all night. Opening the door a crack, she peered cautiously into the hallway and was pleased to find it empty except for her luggage lined up neatly along the wall.

Getting a tight hold on the towel she had wrapped about herself, she was about to grab the nearest case and dart back into the room when a door across the way swung open and

Matt Kirkpatraick stepped out into the hallway.

Fleur froze while his dark-eyed gaze swept the length of her. Though she had managed to catch the hem of the pink towel and whip it about her just in time to prevent complete exposure, Fleur felt as naked beneath the scrutiny of the black eyes as if she wore nothing at all. Amusement flicked on the lips which had so enticed her earlier. "Could I assist you, Miss Normandy?"

Fleur opened her mouth, but no sound came. Spinning about, she plunged into her room, slamming the door behind her.

In less than a second she heard a firm knock, and to her horror saw the door open unceremoniously and brown hands reach in to set a pair of bags firmly inside.

Still clutching the towel to her, Fleur stared speechlessly as the hands withdrew and the door closed behind them. Then she dropped limply onto the bed. The look he had given her in the hall! An unbidden shiver of excitement mingled with acute embarrassment swept over her. Of all the people to make a fool of one's self in front of! What if the pink towel had fallen completely off? What would Matt Kirkpatrick have done then?

What would Fleur Normandy have done!

23

A clatter began in the distance. Fleur sprang up. Josie's triangle! Hastily she flung open the case, snatching a beige denim skirt and a pale green blouse from it. All she needed now was to be late for lunch!

When Fleur rushed into the dining room, Rita and Eric were already seated. Matt Kirkpatrick stood at the window looking out at the pool, but when he heard Fleur's light step and breathless apologies, he turned, his dark eyes fathomless and the mouth which Fleur found so enticing showing no sign of the amusement he had displayed in the hallway.

Fleur felt herself shriveling beneath the sternness of his gaze. Instead of her rumpled skirt and green blouse, was he seeing her naked shoulders above the pink towel?

She sank quickly into the chair opposite Spandell and murmured, "Please forgive me for keeping all of you waiting."

Kirkpatrick said nothing, but took his chair at the head of the table and rang a small pewter bell in the shape of an Olmec head. Josie came at once with a steaming platter which she placed in front of him.

"If we expect to meet out deadlines," said Rita sharply, her green eyes fixed on Fleur, "punctuality will be imperative."

24

"Certainly," murmured Fleur. Across the table Eric Spandell sighed heavily and toyed with a silver fork.

"Miss Normandy had difficulty with her bags." Kirkpatrick spoke tonelessly, but Fleur felt her face flood with color.

"One can always find excuses," replied Rita, but her tone softened as she looked at their host, intent now on serving the plates. The concoction smelled marvelous to Fleur, who had not had a morsel since dinner on the plane the night before, and she soon forgot her unease in watching the deft maneuvering of Kirkpatrick as he lifted the individual servings from the platter.

"Umm! What *is* this?" she could not help exclaiming after the first mouthful. "It's simply delicious."

"*Chiles rellenos,*" replied Kirkpatrick, and Fleur caught a flicker of interest in his dark eyes. "Some people find it too hot the first time."

"Not I! It's perfect." Fleur lifted another forkful of the pepper stuffed with a cheese mixture and chewed appreciatively.

"More tea," said Rita imperiously to a young servant who disappeared instantly and returned almost as quickly with a pitcher.

On the wall opposite Fleur stood a tall curio cabinet in which were displayed a number of metal artifacts, but the item that caught her eye as she ate and held her fascinated was a medium-sized orange bowl on which the colors swirled in varying hues of a most unusual pattern. She turned to Matt. "What an interesting piece on the center shelf. May I ask what it is?"

"Vera Cruz glaze," he replied. Though his expression remained unchanged, his eyes took on a glow as he looked at it. "I treasure it above every other relic I own."

"It's beautiful. And very old, I suspect."

Rita laughed mockingly, but Kirkpatrick seemed to welcome Fleur's interest. "It was discovered in an interior tomb at Chichén where it had lain for several thousand years probably."

Kirkpatrick having dignified Fleur's question with his courteous answer, Rita chimed in. "Vera Cruz pottery was frequently traded in ancient times, but scarcely any of it remains intact today."

"This is the only bowl of its size, I believe," said Matt.

Fleur continued to gaze across the table, totally absorbed. "The mingling of the colors is fantastic."

Eric, whose head was directly in the path of her stare, spoke acidly. "Would you mind

26

examining it at another time, please? I feel like a dragonfly on a pin."

Kirkpatrick laughed.

"I'm sorry!" exclaimed Fleur. "I didn't realize I was boring holes in you." Her attention diverted from the bowl, she watched him helping himself to a delicious-looking green mixture piled on individual lettuce leaves and gracing a white plate. "What is that?"

Eric tasted it. "Avocado-something."

"Guacamole," supplied Matt.

Fleur helped herself. "Is it highly seasoned?"

"Not particularly," said Kirkpatrick. "The avocados are mashed with a bit of onion, tomato, Worcestershire sauce, and salt. The degree of hotness depends on the cook's hand with the Tabasco." He laid aside his fork, and with apparent pleasure watched Fleur eat. "Are you not at all familiar with Mexican cuisine?"

"Oh, I've had a few Broadway enchiladas," she answered with a smile. "But I suspect they were far from the real thing."

"Then you'll get a fine introduction to our cooking from Josie." He resumed eating. "She's an excellent one for innovations as well as traditional dishes."

"Has she been with your family a long

time?" Fleur was beginning to enjoy herself and failed to notice the return of Kirkpatrick's mask of sternness until the silence following her query caused her to look up.

His eyes, now dark coals, burned into hers. "Do you always ask so many questions?"

"Wh – I beg your pardon!" Feeling as if she had been slapped, Fleur turned, crimson-faced to the others. "I hadn't realized... everything is so new and interesting." Her voice died away.

The four of them finished the meal in relative silence, broken only occasionally by Rita's silken remarks to Matt, or Eric's requests to pass something.

Fleur ate without looking up, trying without a great deal of success to concentrate on the piquant flavors of the strange food and to shove aside her burning humiliation. She had apologized no less than three times during the meal, she realized. What a namby-pamby they must all think her! And what a fool she felt. How could she ever learn to get along with these three, whose temperaments were so different from her own? And what on earth had she said wrong to cause Matt Kirkpatrick to turn on her? It was true Rita had warned them not to mention his difficulties with Flaxendon, but she had only questioned him about the cook, for heaven's sake! She suppressed a sigh. Before her, stretching like eternity, lay the months until April.

Finally Matt rose, and the others pushed back their chairs and filed silently into the entry hall where Rita halted, hands on her slender hips, and said imperiously to Spandell and Fleur: "Meet me in the living room at two. We need to map out our strategy."

She turned a winning smile on Kirkpatrick. "Matt has generously agreed to accompany us on our first tour of the ruins, so he'll be meeting with us, too."

So he *was* going to help them! Fleur felt a surge of relief. Even if he was temperamental, he did possess invaluable information. He'd made it quite plain he disliked being questioned, but perhaps once they were in the field, he would supply enough background to make more than a few inquiries unnecessary.

"Shall I bring my equipment to the meeting?" asked Spandell.

"Not today," replied Rita, and then added with a smirk. "I hope *this* time there won't be any difficulties with film."

"Don't worry about it," he answered coolly, and sauntered away toward his room with an easy swagger Fleur envied. An impenetrable armor appeared to be the best defense against Rita Pittman. And probably Matt Kirkpatrick too!

Fighting the temptation of a nap, Fleur decided rather than to risk being tardy again to take a tour of the grounds. She needed to sort out her thoughts anyway before she met again with the other three.

Strolling across the terrace, she paused by the pool, breathing deeply of the still air. Far off in the tangle of thornbushes and rubber trees at the perimeter of the hacienda grounds, she could hear a strange bird calling wistfully. A tide of loneliness rose within her. Never had she been so far away from home. Or in company so hostile.

A low voice coming from directly behind her startled her. "Do you swim?"

Fleur whirled. Matt Kirkpatrick stood a few paces away, hands jammed into his jeans' pockets.

"Yes," she replied hesitantly. "Though I'm not very good at it." How did one make conversation with a man who was friendly one minute and boorish the next?

"I wasn't much of a swimmer myself until a first-rate instructor got hold of me in Dublin."

"Ireland?" Fleur caught her breath as soon as the word slipped past her lips. Questions again! But this time Kirkpatrick seemed unoffended.

"I studied several years in that country. A sentimental journey," he added with a fleet upturning of his mouth. "My father was born there."

More questions crowded Fleur's lips, but she bit them back and turned toward the water. "This pool simply aches to be enjoyed."

She caught his amused glance. "Aches? An inanimate object?"

How literal he was! And why did he so often find it necessary to put other people down? "I often sense emotions in scenes and situations," she answered quietly, turning up a frank gaze. "They're my own, of course, transferred to what I'm seeing."

He was silent for a moment, his dark eyes brooding. "Then you're likely to find the ruins disturbing."

"Am I?" At the moment she was finding Matt Kirkpatrick's nearness disturbing. There was a magnetism in that sensual mouth, the pull of which she found almost irresistible.

"There's unspoken tragedy in Mayan

history, particularly in the case of the cenotes."

"The sacrificial pools." Fleur breathed a prayer of thanksgiving for the sketchy study she had found time for on the plane. "I'm eager to see the relics brought up from them by the air lifts."

His face hardened. "The best ones you won't find in this country. You'll have to go to Philadelphia for that." He turned a cold eye on her. "I understand you're to play the most ludicrous part of all in the nonsense taking place there in April."

Fleur stared. "Nonsense? Do you mean the exhibition?"

"You don't agree the whole idea is ridiculous?"

A rush of anger all but shut off her breath. "I'd hardly be here if I did!" With a tremendous effort she forced calm into her voice. "And what do you mean I'm to play the most ludicrous part?"

He smiled condescendingly. "It's absurd to combine fashion and scholarly research."

Says who? Fleur wanted to scream. The arrogance of the man! "Do you have any idea how Mr. Flaxendon plans to present the artifacts with my designs?"

A glint appeared in his dark eyes. "Please tell me." He motioned toward a bench, and when she took a seat, he sat down beside her.

"The artifacts will be backed by blow-ups of Eric Spandell's photographs," she began. "You see, the whole idea is to present the ruin areas as realistically as possible." Her eyes had begun to sparkle. "So the models wearing the designs will mingle with the viewers as naturally as if they were living in ancient times. The carryover of patterns and colors will be striking. It's a totally original approach and so exciting!"

Kirkpatrick's face was expressionless. "It sounds outlandish to me."

The cameo creaminess of Fleur's flawless complexion deepened. "I see nothing outlandish about it at all! The Mayans were flesh-and-blood people first. *Then* they became the subjects of scholarly research. If it weren't for their art, the ruins would be nothing. If we use our own art to bring them to life again, I say hurrah for that!"

Kirkpatrick seemed amused now. "Do I understand you're classing fashion as art?"

"The best of it is!" snapped Fleur. She had folded her arms militantly under the round curves of her breasts, and her luminous eyes flashed indignantly. For a moment Matt Kirkpatrick studied her; then a slow smile cracked his craggy face. "You're a woman of convictions at least."

Fleur stood up, still annoyed. "We should go in. It's almost two."

"In a moment." His smile vanished as his probing gaze moved over her. "I was abrupt at lunch. I'm sorry."

Fleur's pulse quickened. "I was over-curious," she conceded. "It's one of my failings, I'm afraid."

As if she had not spoken, he went on. "Mrs. Flaxendon brought Josie with her from Cozumel when she married my father. She brought her son as well," he added harshly. "The fashion impresario."

Fleur's lips parted, but she managed to keep silent.

"When Mrs. . . . ." A muscle in his jaw rippled. "Mrs. Kirkpatrick departed with her mercantile-minded offspring, Josie stayed on. It's fair to say she was the only good thing to come out of that fourteen-month fiasco referred to rather asininely by my father as married bliss."

Fleur shivered beneath his intense gaze, and it was with relief she heard the front door open and Rita Pittman call, "Matt! We're waiting."

"Coming." His eyes returned to Fleur, passing up her body and over her face so slowly she felt a wave of giddiness. "I hope your work will go well here."

"Even if you don't approve of it?"

"Perhaps you can change my mind, Miss Normandy."

"If anything is able to do that, Dr. Kirkpatrick," she replied with matching formality, "it will be my designs, not me."

"Really?" He studied her for a long moment. "In only a matter of hours you've already been able to convince me of one thing."

"Oh?" Her brows lifted. "And what is that?"

A glimmer of amusement lit his brooding expression. "That pink is definitely your best color."

Chapter Three

In the living room Rita Pittman had taken a stance of authority in front of the limestone fireplace, and Spandell, who was sprawled on a couch, was gazing around the long, comfortable room whose dark furniture, upholstered in the bright weavings of

35

Mexican artisans, contrasted pleasantly with the starkness of white walls.

A number of fine paintings of the modern European school were hung to the light's best advantage, and on every table and shelf could be seen interesting relics of Dr. Kirkpatrick's profession. It was on one of these that Fleur, her cheeks still burning from the encounter at the pool, fastened her attention, more to avoid meeting the probing gaze of Matt Kirkpatrick seated opposite her than to examine the object. However, her artist's eye was soon absorbed in the swirling design, and in a moment she heard a stage whisper from across the table.

"Plumgate pottery." When her involuntary glance of surprise met Kirkpatrick's, he added with a twinkle, "Guatemalan, late 1600s."

Rita cleared her throat, obviously quite annoyed that Kirkpatrick's undivided attention did not belong to her, though when he entered the room, she had draped herself before the stone hearth in what was plainly a seductive pose. "Shall we begin?"

Kirkpatrick folded his hands at once like an obedient schoolboy, but Fleur saw his lips twitch as he bit back amusement. Perhaps he found Rita's posturing as ridiculous as she did. Fleur glanced quickly at Spandell and found him staring morosely at a tiny cactus

36

growing from the belly of a grinning Mayan god, and bit back her own amusement. What a strange group the four of them made!

Rita spoke sharply. "I'd appreciate your attention, Eric."

Spandell lifted an eyebrow and said in a bored tone, "You'll have it when – or if – you say anything of importance."

Kirkpatrick turned to survey the photographer with mild interest, but made no comment.

Stepping hurriedly into the breech, Fleur said, "We're all eager to hear your plans, Rita."

"Then here they are." Rita fixed a stony gaze on Eric. "For four or five days, possibly a week, Matt will guide us on tours of the major ruins at Uxmal, Chichén Itzá, and Dzibilchaltun, and, if possible, on other side trips."

As she spoke, she transferred her attention to Matt Kirkpatrick and silken flattery quickly replaced her authoritative tone. "This will give us a much needed overview with an opportunity to ask questions of the one man in the world who is best informed concerning the Yucatán."

Matt held her gaze for a moment, and then said in a low voice, "I'm well informed in one or two other areas also."

The blatant suggestiveness of his remark caused Eric to look up sharply and Fleur to stare in shocked fascination at Kirkpatrick's boldness. Rita had asked for it. There was no question of that, but for Matt to respond so pointedly in the presence of others seemed to Fleur in very poor taste.

"And when the week is over," Fleur said, more annoyed than she cared to admit, "what do we do then?"

Matt's gaze swung from Rita to rest lazily on Fleur. "What would you like to do?"

"Return to whatever points of interest apply most specifically to my work," she replied crisply, aware that she sounded like a prudish schoolmarm, but not caring as long as her tone made clear to Matt Kirkpatrick that, unlike Rita, her sole purpose in being here was to tend to business.

"Then that's what you shall do." Matt returned to Rita. "Don't you agree?"

"If our – *designer* would allow me," replied Rita icily. "I was just about to remark that the remainder of our time here we may consider as our own, coming together when necessary to coordinate our work, but free at the same time to pursue our individual work objectives. Is that satisfactory, Miss Normandy?"

"Quite, thank you." Fleur's cheeks

burned, but she felt in complete control of her emotions. "Will transportation be available for going our separate ways?"

"Thanks to Matt, yes," said Rita.

"We have a pickup," said Matt addressing Fleur, "a ranch wagon, and the jeep you and Spendell brought back from Mérida. The wagon isn't much, I'm afraid, but it'll do in a pinch, and if not, there's a car, though its size makes it rather unhandy for the rough going which is sometimes required. And, oh, yes, there's my little roustabout car – if you're really desperate."

Spandell, who had been listening attentively now that they had gotten down to the mechanics of the project, spoke with guarded admiration. "I'd say you're being more than hospitable, Dr. Kirkpatrick. I know the reason for our being here is not quite to your liking." Rita shot him a warning look, but he went ahead. "Yet you're going out of your way to help us. I appreciate that."

"I'm between projects," Kirkpatrick replied, all the earlier playfulness with Rita gone from his voice. "I respect your professionalism. You have a job to do and my being nasty about it won't settle my personal problems."

Fleur felt her annoyance slipping away as

she listened to his quiet voice. Eric was right. He was behaving splendidly to them, even if his mockery of her own part on the project had riled her at the pool.

"However," he went on in harder tone, "I must warn you about one thing. If it were in my power to stop Barry Flaxendon from exhibiting as his own, relics which I consider the property of the Mexican government, I would most certainly do so without a qualm."

Eric studied him for a moment. "But you won't stop us personally. Is that it?"

Kirkpatrick nodded. "If the show must go on, then by all means, let it be a good show."

Fleur shot a triumphant look at Eric: Her estimation of Matt Kirkpatrick's professional feelings about the display of the relics had been correct. Regardless of how he felt personally toward Barry Flaxendon, he was a man of integrity. She could forgive him a great many temperamental outbursts for that.

Aware that he was looking at her, she allowed her gray eyes to meet his dark gaze and was astonished at the intensity with which he was regarding her. What was he thinking? That because of their disagreement over the part fashion should play in a museum showing, she was totally opposed to him?

She smiled tentatively as a signal that she too was willing to put aside personal animosity, and was gratified to see a fleeting upturn of his sensual mouth. She was not so pleased, however, that his smile produced within her chest a sudden crowding. For a dizzy moment she imagined his mouth covering hers, those muscular arms enfolding her, crushing her to the broad chest outlined so appealingly by his close-fitting shirt. Annoyed, she looked away, but when a moment later she could not resist stealing another look at him, her heart knocked unevenly when she found his gaze still fixed upon her.

"Well, what do you think?" Eric Spandell turned over on his back and sat up beside the swimming pool. The late afternoon sun slanted across the clear water and fell warmly on Fleur's shapely legs stretched to dry after a brief swim.

"About the project, you mean?" She spread lotion over her smooth shoulders. "I think it's going to work out fine."

"It could," Eric agreed. "If Rita can keep her paws off Kirkpatrick."

Fleur glanced up quickly. Was that a note

41

of jealousy in Spandell's comment or simply uneasiness about his hopes for success? "What do you mean paws?"

He snorted. "She has a thing for him obviously."

"What if she does?" Fleur remembered Kirkpatrick's dark-eyed gaze. "He seems quite capable of taking care of himself."

"You don't know Rita when she's after a man. She could mess up everything."

Fleur eyed him thoughtfully. "Your last venture with her must have been unpleasant."

"That's a quaint way of putting it. It was sheer hell."

"In what way?"

"Name it," he answered gloomily. "We were at Stonehenge doing a series for Flaxendon. Rita decided she was in love with this English photographer assigned us as an aide, and she set her mind on getting him back to the States. The only way she could swing that was to ruin me in Flaxendon's eyes. She did everything from stealing my film to ripping off cameras to make me look bad."

Fleur waited a moment. "Was she successful?"

"She would have been except for

Flaxendon. He knows her. She was after him once too."

"Yet she's still working for him."

"She's good at her job. Damned good. He keeps her out of his hair by keeping her out of town, but this time she worries me. She's not above using her own resentment of Flaxendon to feed what Kirkpatrick's already got against him. Together they could blow this whole thing."

"But you heard what he said. He won't do anything to stop us."

"But he'd stop Flaxendon if he could," Eric replied glumly. "And little Miss Rita might be the very one to figure out how."

"She wouldn't risk her own career surely!"

Eric's small brown eyes burned hotly. "She'd hardly be doing that, would she, if she allied herself with one of the foremost archaeologists in the continent?"

Fleur felt a sudden chill. Eric was right, of course. Rita and Matt Kirkpatrick could conceivably join forces. Then she and Eric would be out in the cold. He had enough experience and prestige to weather a blow like that, she thought dismally, but this was her first assignment. She'd hardly get another if this one turned out to be a fluke.

She sighed. "I wish there weren't so much

intrigue. And so much animosity between Dr. Kirkpatrick and Mr. Flaxendon."

Eric nodded. "Actually Flaxendon isn't such a bad guy. He knows how to turn a buck, that's all. Matt's a scientist and rich to boot. He doesn't savvy that. He thinks Barry's rotten to the core. The truth of the matter is, the guy's got a lot of respect for culture. That's why he set up the museum." He chuckled. "Well, part of the reason anyway. A tax write-off is the other part, but who isn't looking for tax loopholes these days?

"Anyway," he went on, "at least Flaxendon wants to share the artifacts with the public. He could have just as well socked them away in a bank vault somewhere. If he can make a little extra dough by coordinating the stuff he sells in his store with what the museum displays, I say more power to him for his ingenuity. Unfortunately Matt doesn't see it that way."

Listening to Eric's crass interpretation, Fleur wasn't entirely sure she did either. "Well, I still believe Matt Kirkpatrick meant what he said about helping us. And as for Rita, maybe he –" she swallowed "– maybe he isn't even interested in her."

"She's been here three days," Eric's small,

brown eyes followed a leaf across the pool. "He's interested. If he's human."

Chapter Four

Fleur was not long in finding out that Matt Kirkpatrick was indeed human – too much so perhaps, and that she, to an alarming extent, shared the same quality.

The encounter that proved the fact occurred the fifth day following Fleur's arrival at the hacienda.

All morning the four of them had toured Dzibilchaltun, pacing off the elevated causeway that ran through the ancient city and exploring the Temple of the Seven Dolls, which Fleur found particularly fascinating.

"I want to spend quite a bit more time here," Fleur confided enthusiastically to Kirkpatrick as the two of them were examining some stone carvings. "But I'd be more comfortable if I could at least pronounce the name."

"Then forget about the initial *d,*" he said. "It's that which makes the word so forbidding. Start with the *z*, add that good old American name *Bill,* tack on *chal* and *tune,* and you have it."

"Zee–bill–chal–tune." Fleur smiled up at him. "What a marvelous teacher you are! Now, if I never have to look at it written again, I'll be –"

Without the slightest warning, she suddenly was whisked off her feet and swung abruptly against his taut body. "Tarantula," he murmured, agilely sidestepping the three-inch body of a hairy black spider sunning itself exactly where her next step would have fallen.

Shuddering, she buried her face against his shoulder. "Forget what I said about coming back here."

They were well past the monstrous spider, but still he held her close, and she realized with a quickening heartbeat she was clinging tightly to him too, a fact which – much to her confusion – had nothing to do with the tarantula, but stemmed from a tingling sensation spreading through her like warm wine. Rita and Eric had disappeared behind a grouping of upright stone slabs, and the *mestizo* driver who had accompanied them was nowhere in sight.

Kirkpatrick's dark eyes were so near, Fleur could see within them two tiny reflections of her own oval face and parted lips. He whispered against her cheek. "Tarantulas are relatively harmless, you know."

She felt hypnotized by his stare. "One wouldn't have to bite me," she murmured. "I'd die of fright simply looking at it."

For a long moment their eyes held. Then his arms loosened, and she slid slowly down his thighs until her feet touched the chalky ground. She knew she should walk away from him and break the spell that paralyzed all but her pounding heart but she did not move.

He bent forward. His powerful arms brought her swiftly to him and he took her mouth with his, its urgency igniting all within her she had sought for days to restrain. Spontaneously she matched his passion, and they clung together even after their lips had parted, aware that the curve of their bodies, pressed one against the other, seemed formed for this very sharing.

"I've waited all week for that to happen," he muttered hoarsely.

Then she had not imagined the heat in those dark eyes that had rested upon her so frequently. Her heart pounded. And had he read as well her own gaze, though she herself had been unaware of the messages it sent?

"I - I hope the others didn't see us," she stammered, feeling her face grow hot.

47

Matt Kirkpatrick regarded her with a bemused expression. "Would it matter if they did?"

"They might not understand."

"Then perhaps I don't either."

She swallowed. "What happened was an accident."

"Was it?" She felt his gaze penetrating her, squeezing shut her lungs, arresting her heartbeat.

"The spider –" she faltered.

"Only a catalyst," he murmured. "Don't pretend we haven't longed for each other." He seemed about to take her in his arms again, but this time she moved quickly beyond him, brushing back her lustrous hair nervously, aware that her cheeks were on fire and that she hadn't the faintest idea how to handle the surging emotions raging within her.

From a safe distance she said, "We have work to do."

"Yes." A fierce gleam lit his black eyes, and powerless, she watched his approach. "We've wasted far too much time already." Instantly his mouth covered hers. She felt herself spiraling upward, far above the undulating ground, twirling in a whirlwind of passion. She went limp within his grasp.

48

"Fleur?" He drew back. "What's wrong? What is it?"

She clung weakly to his shoulder.

"Why, you're faint!" He eased her quickly onto a limestone slab. "Here. Rest. I'll be back in a moment."

She closed her eyes gratefully, awash in the waves of longing that had set her head spinning. At once he was beside her again, hovering with a Thermos and a cup of cold water.

"What a fool I am, dragging you around for days in the sun when you've been living like a mole in the city." His arms slipped beneath her shoulders and lifted her toward him for a sip of water.

"I'm all right. Really." *If only he weren't so concerned!*

He let his breath go in an explosive sigh. "I'll take better care of you from here on out, believe me."

"Please don't worry. It's nothing."

"Are you sure?"

She wanted to reach out and erase that worried look, touch those tempting lips – *I must stop this!*

"The truth is, Dr. Kirkpatrick," she said pulling herself upright, forcing a lightness into her tone that rang artificially in the still air, "you overwhelmed me."

49

His expression softened at once. "Did I now?" His lips touched her forehead. "Funny. You have the same effect on me."

Putting on a dazzling smile, she moved away. "That's very nice to hear. But let's let it go at that, shall we?"

His dark brows came together in a puzzled frown.

"You see," she went on quickly with a syrupy pleasantness, "I'm interested only in my work, and I can't very well get it done, can I, if I'm to be distracted in the shadow of every temple and pyramid?"

He regarded her with suddenly narrowed eyes. "A pleasant little peccadillo in the heat of the day." His jaw hardened. "Is that how we're to dismiss what happened just now?"

"Don't you think it's best?"

Some of the warmth left his eyes. "As you say." He got up, taking her arm, but this time no electricity sparked at his touch. "Come. Eric and Rita are waiting lunch."

On a stone slab a few feet from the Temple of the Seven Dolls, Rita had opened the wicker basket packed earlier by Josie and set out a bottle of wine, a variety of sandwiches made with a thick, coarse bread, a plate of assorted fruits, and a smelly cheese, which once past the nose, tasted like manna.

But Fleur found she had no appetite for the delectable picnic and that every morsel that passed her lips tasted exactly the same as the one before it. Her ears, like her tongue, seemed to have lost all sensitivity too, and she listened to the talk around her as if it came from mechanical mouths speaking at a great distance.

"Dzibilchaltun is the only Mayan city never abandoned," Matt said in response to some question of Eric's. "The Mayans were a nomadic people, but this spot was in use almost constantly for at least a thousand years. It was a trade center for the whole hemisphere if the pottery shards are a true indication, which we're certain they are."

"The causeways fascinate me," said Eric. "Constructing them must have been a mammoth job."

Matt nodded. "They were originally built of stone blocks, leveled with gravel, and smoothed with white cement. At the outset they were probably about sixty feet wide."

"But I don't understand their use. Were they simply roadways?"

Rita answered. "This was a temple city. To the Mayans the causeways must have represented something of what boulevards represent to Parisians or Romans."

"Then too, from eight-foot elevations it

51

was easier to keep the jungle at bay," said Matt. "The paved decks which fan out from them once served as supports for the temples."

As he talked, Fleur was aware that his eyes moved impersonally over her face, and she wondered dazedly if she had dreamed those minutes that had left her so numbed. How was it possible for him to regard her so coolly when only a short time ago his touch had been hot with passion?

"Tell me more about the Seven Dolls," said Eric, helping himself to a fat bunch of dark purple grapes.

"I wish I could," said Matt. "About all we know is that in the thirteenth or fourteenth century Indians excavated the temple sanctuary. They dug a hole in the center, plastered the sides, and dropped into it those seven clay dolls I was speaking of earlier, each one with a notable deformity."

"Does such a phenomenon occur in other temples?"

"Not that we've discovered."

"It's thought," interposed Rita, "that the deformities might possibly be related to some sort of healing ritual. Isn't that so, Matt?" Rita's adoring gaze fell on Matt, who returned it with a smile that Fleur found so painful she could scarcely suppress a moan.

As if he felt her anguish, Matt rose abruptly. "If we're going to have time to check out the frieze at the top of the temple and investigate those heaps of stone back in the jungle, perhaps we'd better get started."

Ramon was summoned for the cleaning up, and the four of them set out toward a vine-entangled assemblage of limestone blocks.

"Watch out for tarantulas," said Eric.

Fleur's gaze flew involuntarily to Matt, who responded only by moving ahead, his hand protectively at Rita's elbow.

For the remainder of the afternoon, Fleur wandered about mostly on her own while Eric busied himself with his cameras, and Rita and Matt, professing an interest in some stone projections visible through a tangled mass of greenery farther down the trail, disappeared into the jungle.

I should be glad, thought Fleur, sinking into the shadow of the temple's east side. If it were she instead of Rita alone with Matt, she could not even trust herself to imagine what might be happening. She was well out of it, she assured herself, but deep within her, a nagging loneliness persisted, and she admitted at last that Matt Kirkpatrick's charms could not be cast aside so easily.

Simply thinking about his arms of steel and the thrust of his kiss caused a weakness in her loins she scarcely knew how to cope with. She could not allow herself to indulge her passion, yet how could she ignore it?

She shifted miserably on the warm rock, and it was with intense relief when half an hour later she saw Matt and Rita emerge from a thicket and make their way toward the jeep.

Fleur welcomed the cool breeze whipping against her cheeks on the ride back to the hacienda, and she tried not to notice that Matt's hand, draped casually across the back of Rita's seat, strayed occasionally to her shoulder. Squeezed into the back seat along with Eric, assorted camera equipment, and the empty lunch basket, there was little else to do but think of what had passed between them, however, and finally out of desperation she turned to Eric.

"Did you get some good shots this afternoon?"

"Not many." Eric himself seemed sunk in gloom. "There is one though –" his brown eyes squinted across the horizon "– that might be important."

"Oh?" Fleur forced a smile. "I hope you'll show it to me."

"I will." He turned to look at her. Then in a low voice he said, "But you may wish I hadn't."

Chapter Five

Eric had outfitted a small room off the garage for use as a darkroom, and soon after dinner, he retired there with his film from the day's shooting.

Fleur, too, excused herself, conscious that she could not meet Matt's eyes and had not done so throughout the long, uncomfortable meal.

Selecting a book on the history of Dzibilchaltun from the living room shelves, she went quickly to her room, and after a warm bath, curled up in a lounge chair to study.

The temple history was intriguing and well illustrated but time and again the print on the page blurred, and Fleur caught her thoughts returning to the shadows of that ancient edifice where she had stood locked in Matt's embrace. There was no way to deny, she admitted finally, that she had come away from that encounter emotionally bruised, but hungering still for his touch.

Closing the book with a sharp sigh, she gave herself to the twitterings of sleepy birds in the patio beyond and to the gentle murmurings of the November night. Suppose she did allow herself to think of Matt as more than Dr. Kirkpatrick? Was there any real harm in doing so? He was the most disturbingly attractive man she had ever met, and she had reacted to his caresses as if she were an adolescent schoolgirl, but surely if she became more accustomed to his physical magnetism, his presence would not continue to dissolve her poise.

She quailed, thinking of the flip way she turned Matt aside. What must he think of her, as heated as himself one moment, and the next, an iceberg?

Silly was probably what he thought! Or else that she was a superficial tease.

Which was worse?

Realizing at last that nothing was to be gained by trying to concentrate on ancient events when the problems of the present were so pressing, she abandoned her study altogether and turning out the lamp, went out into the hallway. Tiny niche lights burned at intervals along the walls, and from Matt's study beyond the living room she could see a strip of yellow coming from beneath the door.

Passing through the entry hall, she let herself quietly out into the night. The pool area was lighted indirectly by soft globes burning in the undergrowth, but she kept to the shadows until she came to the low wall adjoining a corner of the house, where she sat down and in a moment was transfixed.

Above her the velvet heavens were hung with a million stars that seemed close enough to touch. Never in the city was it possible to view this amazing panorama, and she stared up at it with deep pleasure while the tenseness that had held her in its grips all afternoon gradually eased. A feeling of peace stole over her. Somehow she would have another chance with Matt, and when it came . . .

Her thoughts broke off at a movement in the shadows just beyond the pool, and in a moment Eric Spandell emerged from the direction of the garage. When he caught sight of her silhouette against the white house, he called out softly, "Fleur? Is that you?"

"Yes." She got to her feet. "I came out for a look at the stars. Lovely, aren't they?"

"I haven't noticed. I've been too busy seeing them in other people's eyes."

Puzzled at his dismal tone, she moved toward him. "What do you mean?"

"Here." He motioned her into the light beside the pool and drew forth a stack of photographic prints from an envelope. "Have a look at these."

The first half dozen or so were of the exterior of the temple, experiments with shadows and light falling on the ancient stones. "These are really fine!" said Fleur, genuinely impressed. Those sharp brown eyes served Eric well!

"But you haven't come to my masterpiece. There!"

Fleur caught her breath. Shining up from the print toward the bottom of the stack were the figures of Matt and Rita, arms entwined, kissing in the foliage.

"What did I tell you?" said Spandell. "She has her hooks in him."

"You shot this today?" Fleur was afraid this time she might truly faint. Surely Spandell had snapped the picture before lunch. Before –

"I took it as we were getting ready to leave Dzibilchaltun. See?" He pointed at the background. "There are those heaps of stone beyond that last ruin we explored."

Matt had gone straight from her lips to Rita's. Fleur felt as if her heart had been

58

squeezed into a throbbing wad of pain. He *was* a devil with women, as Eric had warned. A devil who knew how to cast a pernicious spell. Could one recover from it?

With trembling fingers she handed the prints back to Spandell and said, more for herself than for him, "One kiss needn't mean anything."

He snorted. "I could have taken half a dozen. From what I saw, they'd still be there in that thicket if it hadn't been for us tagging along."

Fleur stared blindly at Spandell. Those moments Matt Kirkpatrick had held her in his arms meant nothing to him. She was only another female. An uncompliant one not worth wasting time on. She wet her lips. "I don't care what they do."

"You'll damn well care if they wreck the exhibition!"

"They won't do that." Was that tremulous thread of sound her voice? "They'll –" Her words stuck in her dry mouth. "They'll be too absorbed in one another."

"Maybe," said Spandell. "Let's hope to God it works out that way. If he can keep her satisfied..."

"Don't!" cried Fleur sharply. Then in a lamer tone, "Don't worry about it."

"That's good advice." He sauntered past

her. "For fools. We shut our eyes to this, and we may wake up one morning minus a job."

"I think you're dramatizing what you saw way out of proportion." If only she could believe that! If she could turn back time, have another chance to respond to Matt as she had wanted to . . .

"Dramatic, is it?" Spandell turned at the foot of the path and looked back at her. "We'll see. At any rate, I guess there's nothing we can do about it tonight. Are you coming in?"

"In a minute."

He went on, leaving her to stare silently up at the stars and to wonder how, in the presence of such glory, she could feel such unrelenting pain.

For nearly an hour Fleur remained in the shadows near the pool while over and over she played the events of the day: Matt's kiss, her own heated response followed by the coldness that had sent him straight to Rita's arms: Spandell's picture and his claim that the photographed embrace was only one of many.

For a time the misery produced by this recounting blurred her thinking, but gradually a part of her agony eased. She had experienced emotional trauma this day, and it had shaken her, but it had not destroyed her.

Only a foolish, immature person would allow a couple of kisses from a comparative stranger to turn her world upside down. True, for a few seconds listening to Eric and looking at the print had devastated her, but she was all right now and able to view the situation logically and objectively.

Matt Kirkpatrick was an egotist of the first order who amused himself by adding conquests to some tally sheet of females fallen victim to his rugged good looks, his money, his power in scientific circles.

But she refused to be counted in that number.

Of far greater interest to her than a pair of strong arms and a persuasive kiss was the satisfaction she got from creating interesting, original designs. This trip to the Yucatán was offering her a unique opportunity to make her mark, and nothing must be allowed to deter her from that goal.

Bolstered by new resolutions and an hour alone in the darkness, Fleur made her way back to the house, opening the door softly and letting herself in without a sound.

She intended to go directly to her room, but glancing into the dining room, she was startled to see the curio cabinet standing wide open and beside it Matt, bent over the table with his back toward the door.

If she tried to slip by unnoticed, she would feel like an intruder evading a night watchman, but to make herself known would mean having to face Matt, an encounter she felt not quite up to handling.

She hesitated a moment too long.

Sensing a presence, Matt turned and saw Fleur frozen like some wild creature of the night caught suddenly in a headlight beam.

"Fleur!"

"I've been out looking at the stars."

He gazed, unblinking. "Our nights are quite impressive."

"It's the clear air, I suppose."

"Yes."

What an inane conversation! Fleur longed to move on but felt herself rooted to his unrelenting stare.

"What are you doing?" she said finally, aware that it was none of her business, but desperate for some way to break the spell which held her motionless.

He cast a backward glance at the table, then lifted from it the object of his perusal. "I was examining this piece of Vera Cruz pottery."

He held up to the light the orange bowl

Fleur had so admired during their first meal together. "Just now I remembered a ridiculous dream I had last night." A sheepish grin swept away his sternness. "I had to come at once and make certain that's all it was – a dream, and nothing more."

"You thought something had happened to the bowl?"

"According to the dream it was smashed in a dozen pieces."

"But it's all right, isn't it?" She was surprised at her own sense of anxiety.

He smiled again. "See for yourself."

Cautiously she took it from his outstretched hand and turned it slowly in her own, admiring the blending of yellows and browns that resulted in the rare shades of swirling color. "A marvelous technique produced this." She fixed her eyes intently on its undulating brightness. "So elusive!" Lifting her eyes suddenly, she said, "I wonder if I could . . ."

She broke off at once, color rising to her cheeks.

Matt looked down at her. "Could what?"

"Never mind." Quickly she handed the bowl back to him. "It wasn't a good idea. But I do want to ask if someday when I have the time I might come in here and study it."

For a moment he regarded her without

speaking. Then he said quietly, "You'd accomplish more if you took it to your room where you could work with it at leisure."

Fleur's color deepened. "No, really." If only she could explain her sudden vision of that exotic orange in a skirt of shimmering chiffon! "It's true I did think for a second of a prolonged study. I'd like to try reproducing those color tones in a fabric. But the bowl is far too precious to be removed from its case for any length of time."

In the soft light of the dining room, her fresh young skin, made more rosy by the awkwardness of the moment, had taken on an appealing luminescence pointed up by the lustrous dark hair that framed her face.

When Matt Kirkpatrick found his voice again, he said impulsively, "Take it. Please! Keep it as long as you like."

Fleur stared, amazed. "I wouldn't dare risk having your dream come true!"

"Nonsense."

"But it could, you know."

His tantalizing lips curled. "Could you be so careless?"

"Not intentionally, but accidents do happen."

"I trust you."

The simple statement accompanied by a penetrating gaze she felt to the soles of her feet reduced her protests to mere murmurings. "You're certain?"

"Absolutely." He pressed the bowl into her hands, and at his touch the wall of logic she had erected beneath the stars gave way under a fresh flood of desire. Her knees turned to jelly.

Setting the bowl carefully upon the table, she put out a hand to steady herself. "This wood. I've been meaning to examine it."

"Zapote wood," Kirkpatrick tapped the tabletop lightly. "It's extremely hard. You'll see it in the temple carvings."

"I did this morning." *Before you kissed me.* She went on in a rush. "Is it still available?"

He nodded. His gaze was fixed upon her, his lips parted. Was he remembering too?

Her words tumbled over each other. "I think it might work up very well in beads and in carvings for pins."

The softness vanished from his lips and surliness replaced it. "You never swerve from your devotion to duty, do you?"

Stunned by the unexpectedness of his rebuke, she answered coldly, "Hardly ever."

"It's interesting that you are able to take so seriously the whims of silly women who live only for changing hemlines and the latest fads." His voice was as icy as his stare.

"If you don't mind, I'd rather not discuss a subject on which you are so blindly biased."

"You sidestep nicely."

She marched swiftly to the door. "Good night, Dr. Kirkpatrick."

"Wait." His low voice halted her. "The bowl." He held it out to her. "You've forgotten it."

She crossed the room in a martial stride, but as she took it from his, their hands touched once again, and for a moment neither moved. At the base of Matt's throat Fleur saw a tiny pulse gone wild, and her own head spun.

With enormous effort she pulled her gaze away.

"Sleep well," he said softly when she reached the door again. She did not reply though every nerve in her body willed her to look back, to find again in the depths of Matt Kirkpatrick's brooding eyes her own reflection and an assurance that she, not Rita Pittman, lived within them.

Chapter Six

The days following Fleur's encounter with Matt in the dining room went swiftly by. Though she had expected Matt to leave the Flaxendon team to its own resources after conducting the initial tours of the ruin sites, he continued to lead them daily to more remote spots that those less well acquainted with the area could not possibly have found.

Listening to his low voice explaining the customs and daily life of the Mayans and the Toltecs was an enriching experience for Fleur, and she gave herself to it with complete concentration, forcing from her mind any thoughts of what the attractive man speaking so eruditely meant to her as a woman. But at night she was not so fortunate.

As soon as she had put away her work and turned out the light, he emerged from the subconscious vault that she had suppressed him to and proceeded to resume the postures of the day, his warm voice moving over the strange Mexican names with a melting resonance that caused her to toss restlessly and clasp her pillow to her breast.

When she did finally manage to drop off to sleep, there he was again, in all her dreams, not as the aloof and reserved lecturer, but as a lover who gathered her in his arms and set fire to her desires. More than once she woke up blissfully, his name on her lips, only to realize with shattering disappointment that what had brought her such pleasure had not happened and never would.

For it had become increasingly evident as the days passed that Rita Pittman had indeed set her sights on Matt Kirkpatrick who in turn seemed not in the least opposed to her ploys for his attentions and when she insinuated her svelte figure into positions that invited his touch, he made no effort to avoid her. In response, she turned on him looks of such sultry promise that even Spandell dropped his glance in embarrassment.

After each such display, Fleur burned with shame that she herself had ever entertained romantic illusions about their host. His whole manner with Rita disgusted her, and she resolved anew each time to have nothing further to do with him beyond what was required to accomplish her work.

How could she ever have been deceived by those black eyes in which she had seen her own face reflected? He was a practiced Romeo, reveling, no doubt, in the illusion that she had fallen under his spell. Thank goodness she'd had sense enough to draw back in time!

But the moments she was able to content herself with these arguments were short lived, and she soon realized with a sickening sense of self-betrayal that she missed intensely those searching looks from Matt's dark eyes. For the truth was, not since the night in the dining room had he once sought her out or paid any more notice to her than he did to Spendell.

At first she convinced herself that she was relieved. If he were ever to realize the extent of his attraction for her, she dared not think how he might take advantage of that realization. But another less logical part of her felt slighted each time she saw his eyes moving over Rita or his brown hand curved about her waist, so it was with a sense of release she greeted Rita's announcement at Friday night's dinner that the four of them would gather in the living room following the meal to discuss their individual projects and work out some sort of schedule for the use of the vehicles at their disposal.

The group trips were finished then.

Good, thought Fleur. Once off by herself she could get over this pointless attachment to a man who plainly cared nothing for her. Her feelings for him were strictly physical anyway, she reminded herself, and dependent for their survival upon the sight of his muscular leanness, tantalizing mouth, and engaging glances.

Alone, she could immerse herself in her work, and within a few days would be able to laugh at the foolish way her heart knocked at the mere sight of Matt Kirkpatrick.

"As you know," said Matt when they were gathered in the library over coffee, "you have available to you at all times the jeep, the ranch wagon, and the pickup."

"Don't forget the car," Rita purred from the couch where she sat, legs curled beneath her, full lips parted. "The Cadillac, I mean."

Everyone had seen the expensive white automobile in one of the garages, and periodically Ramon backed it out and polished it with pride, but Matt had never been seen driving it, and Fleur had somehow felt he eschewed its use as ostentatious. Now she discovered there was rather more to it than that.

Matt, usually so compliant where Rita was concerned, spoke coldly. "The Cadillac was my father's. It has its purpose, but touring ruins isn't one of them. You are, of course, welcome to use my car in the event one or the other of the vehicles I've already mentioned is tied up."

Matt's car, surprisingly enough for the debonair bachelor image he projected, was a ramshackle old Ford which, no matter how often Ramon washed and polished it, still refused to shine.

"I think you're being most generous," said Fleur, put off by Rita's greediness. "Certainly the three of us can manage with three means of conveyance."

Rita eyed her coldly and lit a cigarette. "I'll be using the pickup tomorrow."

Matt's gaze, which had rested briefly on Fleur as she spoke, now moved to Rita. "What are your plans?"

"I'm going over Chichén with a fine tooth comb." Fleur watched her seductive exhalation of spiraling smoke rings. "I want pictures from every angle of El Castillo. I want the Chac-mools, the ball court, the works." She looked coolly across at Eric. "You'll need a good night's sleep. I'm going to put you through the mill tomorrow."

Eric, who had seemed scarcely to be

71

listening, so absorbed was he in tinkering with a camera in his lap, lifted his head and spoke absently. "Why not put off going until Monday?"

"It's Chichén tomorrow!" snapped Rita.

Eric shrugged. "Suit yourself, but if we wait until I process the film I've taken already at that site, we might save ourselves some duplication."

"We're going tomorrow, and that's that."

"Fleur?" Matt turned to face her, and the tremor his glance always inspired seized her. "Where will you be going?"

"Since transportation isn't a problem," she answered, carefully controlling her voice. "I'll take the jeep into Mérida. One of the books I've been studying mentions an outstanding exhibit of ancient jewelry in the museum there. I'd like to have a look at it before I complete my own designs."

"Good." Matt crossed to the table and refilled his cup. "More coffee anyone?" He set the pot back on the table and returned to take a seat beside Rita. "I'm going to Mérida myself on a business matter. I can drive you."

Rita's sharp intake of breath could be heard throughout the room, and for an awful moment Fleur was afraid she herself was responsible for the sound. An entire day alone with him? She could never manage that!

Rita, too, shared Fleur's displeasure. "I'd planned on your going with me to Chichén," she said to Matt. Though her tone was sweetly coaxing, there was steel beneath it.

"Eric will be with you."

"Eric!" Rita gave a deprecating laugh, and Fleur saw Spandell flinch. "He takes nice pictures, but not always of the right subjects."

"See here, Rita!" Spandell sat forward on his chair, a white line circling his tight mouth. Had he shown Rita the picture he had taken of her and Matt? And if so, why? Fleur wondered.

"I can use Matt's guidance as well as you can," Rita said placatingly, realizing she had gone too far. Spandell was an excellent photographer and would brook no snide remarks concerning his professional ability, no matter whether his subject was a pair of lovers or a three-thousand-year-old temple.

"Won't you come?" Rita linked her arm possessively with Matt's.

Matt shook his head. "Not tomorrow."

"Isn't it too bad," said Eric with oily amusement, "that Chichén can't wait until Monday."

Rita shot him a look of pure hatred, and

73

then turned her angry gaze on Fleur who was shifting uncomfortably under a question from Matt.

"Can we leave as early as seven?"

Fleur wondered if she could speak past her pounding heart. Now was the time to find some graceful way to change her plans. Rita's furious face was warning enough that going off alone with Matt was an impossible idea, and her own feelings confirmed that opinion.

But she did need to make the trip. If she waited until the next week to go, the ideas teeming now inside her head might cool beyond usefulness.

"Seven?" She heard her voice from a long way off. "I'll be ready."

"I'm sure of *that!*" said Rita in an acid tone.

Eric grinned lazily and rose. "You can count on me, too, dear Rita. All you have to do is call."

Chapter Seven

Thirty minutes away from the hacienda on the road to Mérida, Matt glanced across at Fleur. "Did you have a chance

74

to see much of the city when you arrived?"

"Hardly any of it." Uneasily she pulled her attention from the misty green fields of hennequen, a cultivated variety of cactus from which strong sisal fiber was derived and which, Matt had explained, had formed the basis of his father's fortune. "Eric picked me up at the airport, and we drove straight from there to the hacienda."

She cast a wary look at his craggy profile. Did he really have business in Mérida or had he used that as a trumped-up excuse to provoke another scene like the one which had occurred at Dzibilchaltun? "I do remember wondering about all the windmills, though," Fleur remarked.

Matt chuckled. "Something I imagine you scarcely expected in Mexico. But they're here on the peninsula for a good reason. You're aware, I suppose, that there is no surface water here?"

"No rivers?" Fleur stared.

"That's right." He smiled. "No babbling brooks, no lakes, nothing of that sort."

"But why not?"

"Look at the land. Porous limestone. Whatever rain we get seeps through to a solid rock base, then flows into underground rivers. Those are really what you are seeing in the cenotes. Underground streams which show up when the limestone cracks and forms wells."

As he spoke, his detached air reassured her. There was nothing to be alarmed about after all. The thoroughly agreeable man at the wheel was completely absorbed in his pride in this land to which his Irish father had emigrated and which he had eventually subdued into an immensely profitable partner.

"If the windmills in Mérida are pumping private water supplies," she said, relaxing, "why don't you have them at the hacienda?"

"We did until recently. My father installed electric pumps when I was a boy, but he left the windmills as a source of water for the stock, and for local color." A change came over his face and sent his smile scudding behind a cloud of sudden displeasure. "Mrs. Flaxendon was of the opinion they clashed with the grandeur of the surroundings. They were taken down."

The two of them rode in silence for a while, Fleur pondering the bitterness that any mention of his father's second wife or her son invariably produced. What had his own mother been like, she wondered. Was she Spanish? Or *mestizo* – that happy blend of Indian and Spanish that had evolved in the

76

fine-boned inhabitants that her aesthetic senses reacted to so pleasurably whenever she saw them in the streets or on the way to the ruins.

Fleur looked across at the lithe, muscular figure at the wheel and felt the strength emanating from the broad shoulders and thick neck that supported his chiseled profile. There had never been a strong man in her life, either physically or spiritually. What was this one like when he was not the lecturer or the lover, she wondered, but simply a man?

She sighed, saddened. There were so many things she longed to know about Matt Kirkpatrick, and now she never would. Soon her work would be finished here. She glanced quickly at him, and then away as quickly, frightened by the rush of emotions the thought of never seeing him again aroused.

Willing her attention to focus on the passing landscape, she said, "What crop is this? Corn?"

Matt nodded. "Along with frijoles, it's the staple food for the natives. Maize it's called here. An accidental cross between wild grasses thousands of years ago produced it."

Fleur made a mental note to include the gracefully waving stalks in a design. Perhaps on a border print. The idea set her thoughts going in a new direction and a full five minutes passed before an awareness of Matt's eyes upon her brought her back to the jeep with a start.

Matt glanced away just in time to avoid running off the road. "If I'd brought repellent, we could stretch our legs a bit in the fields." His gaze came back to her, different now, she noted with a lurching heart. There were questions in his dark eyes. Did he wonder about her too?

"We mustn't ignore the ticks, must we?" she murmured, grateful for once to the *garrapatas,* which on more than one occasion had managed to skip past her precautionary smearings of citronella and bury themselves in the soft flesh of her thighs. She scarcely dared think what a walk in a cornfield at the side of Matt Kirkpatrick might have on her now. She was not at all sure she could resist inviting that tantalizing mouth to taste her lips once again.

He spoke as if he read her thoughts. "For Mexicans, maize holds an erotic symbolism. Phallic worship is inherent in the cultural beginnings of this area." His low-pitched voice warmed her alarmingly. "They believe man was originally made from corn."

Fleur tore her eyes from his. "What are those tiny houses every so often among the

78

rows?" Heaven knew what they might be, but surely not anything more embarrassing than Matt's discourse on primal instincts when her own instincts were so aroused!

"The season's first ears of corn are placed there," he answered.

"Why?"

"To feed the *alux*, the little people."

"Elves, you mean?" Her discomfort vanished, her whole attention caught up in this enticing new idea.

He nodded, seemingly pleased at her delight. "Or leprechauns, as the Irish say. The peasants believe if the *alux* are fed well, they reciprocate by pushing up the ears of corn. They may even rock your hammock while you sleep."

Fleur leaned toward him excitedly. "How fascinating universal lore is! Why, that belief almost exactly parallels the Nordic one of the brownie cobblers. Do you remember?" Her eyes sparkled. "In the evening, as I recall, one leaves out milk and bread, and while one dreams, his shoes are mended."

Matt looked at her flushed cheeks and gray eyes shining above them. Returning his gaze to the road, he said quietly, "Do you have any idea how beautiful you are?"

This low-voiced praise caught Fleur completely off guard. "Why – thank you."

"You're so fresh, so exuberant. So overflowing with the life force." His puzzled tone seemed directed more to himself than to her, almost as if he were some sort of scientist who, while dissecting specimens in a laboratory, had turned up a rare mutant.

"Most of the women I've known," he went on, "have been empty. Shells, waiting for some man to fill them with life's goodies." A bleakness took hold of him, and when he turned to look at her, she saw the sparks had faded from his eyes, leaving burned-out coals set in a stern face. "I try to steer clear of women."

"Oh?" Fleur had a sudden vision of Eric's photograph of Matt and Rita embracing. "I hadn't noticed."

He went on speaking with no sign that he had heard her. "I can't believe I was once naive enough to think happiness meant finding a wife, making a home, having children."

Fleur blinked. How was it possible that only a few moments before the two of them had been pleasantly engaged in a conversation about elves, and now this disturbing man was baring his soul to her! Fleur's lips parted. "And what do you believe now?"

His answer came back at once cloaked in

desolation. "That to be happy on this earth is the dream of a fool."

Fleur caught her breath. "You don't mean that!"

"Don't I?" His glance flicked over her. "Then suppose you tell me – what's the point of it all?"

"Of living?" Fleur stared. "What's the point of living?"

"Yes!" The word rang with challenge. "You've seen the ruins. Millions of Mayans and Toltecs lived and died and that's all that is left of them. Stone slabs, carved beasts, crumbling temples."

Fleur continued to stare, unbelieving. "But you're one of the foremost archaeologists of this hemisphere! How can you talk like that."

"Perhaps the fact that I've spent my whole adult life tracking down lost civilizations is the very reason I do talk like that." His voice dropped to a murmur. "What do all those civilizations amount to? Mankind is no better off for all those creatures who once roamed the earth. They made love and gave birth and died." He turned a steely look in her direction. "So what?"

"You," she whispered. "You're the one who is empty!"

"Perhaps I am." His voice came back at

81

her harshly. "Well, never mind. It doesn't matter."

"But it does!" Fleur sat forward on the edge of her seat. "You can't seriously mean what you've just told me."

"That there's no point to living?" He was silent for a moment, his black eyes fastened on the unbending road ahead. "Well, there's pleasure, of course." His tone held a hard edge. "One can lose oneself in that for a time."

"Self-gratification, you mean." Making love to Rita and women like her. Fleur's heart hammered. "You can't mean you've found nothing beyond that which truly satisfies you."

He hesitated. "Only one thing."

Fleur wondered if she dared delve deeper into the secret thoughts of this man who held so much attraction for her and so much power over her own happiness. "What?"

"My work. The preservation of the scraps of all that has gone before."

"Preservation!" Disappointment all but choked Fleur. "That's all that matters? Picking up the pieces?"

"God knows there are enough of them around," he answered with bitterness.

"But what about creating?" To drop the subject at once would be wise, she knew, but

Fleur was too incensed by Matt's blithe dismissal of all she held to be dear to let it go without an argument. "What about wholeness? Newness?"

"I haven't the faintest idea what you're talking about."

"I'm talking about taking what we find in this world and shaping it into something new. Putting our mark upon it!"

"What for? Nothing lasts," he answered.

"So why bother? Is that what you think?"

"Exactly!" He shot her a fierce look which turned swiftly to surprise, then to laughter. "I wish you could see your face. You're red as a beet!"

"Only because I'm furious!" she snapped. "And how dare you laugh at me when you're the one who started the whole ruckus in the first place!"

He pulled to the side of the road and turned off the motor. "You are really angry, aren't you?"

Fleur felt hot tears ready to spill. "You're the most stupid man I've ever known!"

Ignoring the insult, he stared at her, puzzled. "But why? Why are you so furious?"

Fleur wanted to hit him. "I've just told you! Don't you listen to anything?"

A strange look came over his face. "You're angry because you care what I think," he said slowly. "In spite of that prissy little speech you made at Dzibilchaltun you haven't been able to dismiss me from your thoughts any more than I've been able to get you out of mine, though God knows I've tried." His arms pulled her roughly to him and crushed her against his chest. "Fleur," he muttered hoarsely. Then his lips were covering hers with a fierce exploring urgency.

She struggled only a moment, then yielded to the flood of passion his warm mouth had freed, lifting her lips to him like ripe fruit, joyously, her anger spent like so much smoke.

"Someone will come along," she whispered shakily when his mouth had finally moved to her temple, his hands to the nape of her neck.

She felt his words inside her ear. "Why do you always bother so about what other people think?"

"Everything matters to me," she said.

He drew away and looked tenderly down at her. "Is that the source of your exuberance? Caring?"

"I don't know." She looked away, confused, her emotions still turbulent. "I only know life is too wonderful to be dismissed as boring or –" she drew a breath "– or meaningless."

His eyes touched every part of her face. "Could you teach me to care that much?"

If only she could answer *yes!* "Everyone learns that for himself."

"Do you think I can?"

"Do you want to?"

He was silent, his eyes still moving over her face. Then sliding back across the seat, he started the motor and eased the jeep back onto the road.

For miles they rode in silence while armies of misgivings swarmed through Fleur's brain. How preachy and disgustingly arrogant she must seem to him! Why hadn't she simply reveled in his embrace and let it go at that?

But letting things go wasn't her style, she thought with a sigh. Why was it she always seemed to demand perfect accord between herself and those she loved and couldn't rest until she had it?

Those she loved?

She brought herself up sharply. What nonsense! Matt Kirkpatrick had kissed her twice and she thought herself in love. She cast a wistful look across the seat. Still, no man's lips had ever made her feel as his had.

She had all but given up hope of another

word being exchanged between them when his voice, breaking suddenly into her thoughts, startled her like gunfire.

"I'm sorry if I've upset you with my gloom."

"Oh, don't apologize! I think it's good we've..." She bit her lip. With Matt it was so easy to say the wrong thing. "We've gotten to know each other better."

He smiled. "I like what I know."

"So do I." But that wasn't entirely true, she thought at once. She hated the quicksilver changing of his moods, his unexpected flashes of anger. She fastened her gaze on passing fields of maize and small adobe houses with thatched roofs reaching sharply toward the sky. "But, of course, I really don't know you."

He smiled wickedly. "My name is Matthew St. Gawain Kirkpatrick."

When she turned quickly to look at him, his mouth curved up so invitingly it was all she could do not to lean over and place her own mouth lovingly against it.

"I was born in Mérida and educated in Dublin," he continued in the tone one might use in an office interview. "Later I studied at Cambridge and went on to work in New York."

Was I there? Fleur wondered. *Did we pass*

86

on the street, and I didn't even know you?

"I was with the Museum of Natural History for a time." A shadow crossed his face. "I was never happier, never more alive than in those days."

"Of course," she said quietly. "You were sharing."

He looked at her. "What do you mean?"

"I mean that what you'd learned you were using to help others learn. To bring other people the same joys and satisfactions you'd found."

He said nothing, and she leaned toward him. "That's the reason the Flaxendon Exhibition is going to be so wonderful, Matt," she said eagerly. "Ordinary people are going to have a chance to see the Mayans as they really were. They'll be participating in a living culture, and through the clothes and jewelry I design, they can even own a part of it."

She saw at once by the closed look which came over his face she had gone too far. "Matt? You do see, don't you?"

"I see Mérida up ahead." All the warmth had vanished from his voice; his chin jutted stubbornly. "And just in time," he finished grimly.

Chapter Eight

Matt's voice was raised over the roar of the motor. "I'll meet you at four in front of the Rozo Monument."

Fleur scarcely had time to step out onto the sidewalk before the jeep began to move away. "Wait!" she called angrily. "Where is it?"

"Just down the street a few blocks," he flung back with impatience. "Ask anyone."

The jeep turned a corner while Fleur stared stonily after it. The last fifteen minutes of their ride into Mérida had seemed an eternity. Neither of them had spoken except in monosyllables until they reached the outer limits of the city. Then Matt had inquired icily which museum she wanted to visit. When she replied that she knew of only one, he had turned such a withering look of condescension upon her that she would gladly have gotten out then and there and found her own way.

Glancing about now, she saw that Matt's was the only vehicle in the least hurry. For a city street, this one was certainly sleepy. Little two-wheeled horse-drawn *calesas* moved slowly along carrying relaxed businessmen to their appointments. Pedestrians ambled along the sidewalks gazing into shop windows, and from a second-story balcony a man with a guitar sang a mournful ballad.

She should never have mentioned the Flaxendon Exhibition, of course. Or at least not her part in it, she thought miserably, pausing before the entrance to the museum. The idea of mixing culture and merchandising enraged Matt, and she knew that. Why had she brought it up again then? *She* was the one who was stupid.

Her face burned at the remembrance of having used that term on Matt. But he was so smug in his hopelessness! So infuriatingly numb to the wonders all about him. His soft life had left him insensitive and unable to appreciate the feelings of others. What he needed was a few hard knocks!

Suddenly she was aware of the curious stares of passersby and realized her face must be beet red again, and perhaps she might even have been talking to herself! Hurriedly she ducked into the museum, glad for its shadowed corridors where she might have a moment to recover her poise.

Once she laid eyes on the cases filled with the treasures of the cenotes, however, she forgot everything else. There were whimsical little idols of rubber and wood, bone knives wrapped in gold foil, jade portraits, gold-plated beads, ceramic masks, death bells, earplugs. Her fingers fairly itched to draw, and soon she found an isolated bench before the largest of the cases and settled herself, not to copy, but to unleash the wealth of ideas the artifacts had stimulated.

For hours she sat there, but to Fleur they flew by like minutes. She did not see the curious glances of other museum visitors or hear their hushed murmurs of *"artista."* She saw only the magical confluence of the Mayan designs and her own, mingling in swirling skirts, ornate print blouses, sophisticated pins, and yards of necklaces. She heard only the music of the wind whistling through the broken temple walls, the thousand-year-old cries of maidens drowning in the sacrificial wells.

Finally there was a gentle voice at her shoulder. "Closing, *señorita.*" She jumped up with a start.

"What time is it?"

"Five, *señorita.*"

Five! She snatched up her sketch pad and purse. "The Rozo Monument. Where is it?"

90

"You go three blocks to the north, please." The guard beamed and kissed his fingertips. *"Es muy hermosa, señorita, muy simpática."*

"I'm sure it is beautiful and charming." Fleur flashed a smile and dashed past him. "And I'm also sure I'm terribly, terribly late!"

Out in the street, the sun was still high, and she stared in confusion through the white light. North. Which way was that?

Starting off in a gallop toward her left, she breathed a silent prayer that this was the right way. Matt had been so angry when he let her out he might even have gone off and left her.

But in a few minutes her anxiety was forgotten when rearing up ahead was the most spectacularly carved monument she had ever seen.

An Indian woman of heroic proportions dominated the center of it, and wound about her bosom were serpents. As Fleur drew nearer, she could see in the outstretched arms of the statue a plaque of heraldry and carved below this a thatched hut in which votive lights burned. On both sides were masses of rugged symbols and figures which built all the way up to the central height.

Matt forgotten, Fleur peered up at the

convolutions in fascination. There were heads, hands offering bread, corn, buildings, statues of gods, all in a glorious conglomeration. Extending back in a semi-circle, the sides of the monument were covered with other carvings commemorating the laws and reforms of hundreds of years past.

Awestruck, Fleur walked slowly around the semi-circle, discovering at every step more intricacies: trees, butterflies, an eagle wrestling with a fire-breathing serpent.

All at once she felt her arm gripped firmly and heard an anxious voice in her ear. "Where were you?"

Whirling, she discovered Matt staring intently down at her. Fleur blinked. Was this worried-looking man the same one who had so unceremoniously dumped her in front of the museum a few hours ago? "I'm so sorry I'm late."

"Never mind. You're here now." Why, he was actually smiling!

At the sight of those lips turned up so appealingly, Fleur's heart lifted. "Matt, this monument!" She waved at the edifice towering over them. "I had no idea there was anything so impressive in Mérida."

"That's why I wanted us to meet here." Matt lifted his eyes. "It is quite astonishing, isn't it?"

"But what does it all mean?"

"The Indian is Mother Earth; the serpents, wisdom and fertility." He still had hold of her arm, and now he guided her slowly around the monument, his low voice thrilling her almost as much as his touch. "The heraldry is the Yucatecan coat of arms. Those two jaguar-headed human figures crouching in worship signify courage."

They had come back in front of the monument again. "It's a history actually," he concluded.

"And such a detailed one!"

He smiled down at her. "Where were you so long? I was afraid you were lost."

"I was. In the museum," she added hastily. "I forgot everything. Just wait until you see my drawings." She had already fetched her sketchbook from beneath her arm when she remembered their quarrel. "Oh, never mind," she said quickly. "They won't interest you."

"Don't be too sure." Then at her look of surprise, "I was a little lost, too, but I've had an hour to get my bearings."

"I'm so sorry I kept you waiting," she said again.

"Forget it. What I want to know now is where you had lunch."

At her blank look, he shook his head in

93

mock despair. "Don't tell me you forgot lunch, too."

"I'm afraid I did."

"You haven't had a bite since breakfast?"

She shook her head.

"Come along then," he said briskly. "We'll remedy that." His firm grip left no alternative and soon they were settled in a dimly lit restaurant at a corner table where Fleur could view the quaint Mexican handicrafts decorating the walls and listen to the somnolent whispers of the soft-spoken natives at other tables.

"What will you have?" said Matt. In the shadowed interior, his dark features blended in a warm glow that centered in his eyes and lent an extra softness to his enticing mouth.

"Whatever you say."

"Turkey cooked in a rather complicated sauce is the specialty of the house."

"Then by all means let's have that." There was an air of unreality about the place, Fleur thought, and about her being here with Matt Kirkpatrick, particularly after the stormy finish of their morning ride. Even if he had not left her stranded, as she had half feared hurrying from the museum, she had expected him to usher her in a fury to the jeep and hasten back to the hacienda. She looked about the pleasant little room where

94

soft music created a romantic backdrop and delightful smells issued from the kitchen. What a pleasant surprise it all was!

"*Mole poblana de guajolote*," Matt said to the Mexican waitress attired in a lace-edged peasant blouse and full skirt which fell almost to the huaraches covering her small brown feet. "And margaritas. A tequila drink," he said in explanation to Fleur. "I think you'll enjoy it."

"Tequila. That's cactus juice, isn't it?"

"A rather fiery version of it, yes."

"I like hot things."

He surveyed her evenly. "So I noticed the first night we met."

Fleur shifted uneasily. "The *chiles rellenos*, remember?"

"Oh, yes!" For a moment she thought he meant to bring up the boiling resentment she had tried rather unsuccessfully to hide when he rebuked her for asking so many questions, but looking across at him she saw that particular unpleasantness as well as whatever anger he had felt toward her when they arrived in Mérida was forgotten now in the serenity of the moment.

"Was your business meeting a success?" she asked as the waitress set before them two frosted glasses rimmed with salt.

95

He sighed. "With lawyers, it's hard to tell sometimes."

Lawyers! Oh, dear. She had brought up the Flaxendons again! She was about to broach a quick change of subject when he went on in a musing tone.

"I suppose I ought to simply give in gracefully and get the thing settled once and for all."

"But you don't really want to?" she ventured carefully.

"It isn't a case of wanting to so much as that I feel doing so would be a betrayal."

"I'm afraid I don't understand," she murmured.

"Flaxendon can have the house or the whole hacienda if he wants. I couldn't care less about that, but I do care that he's pirated relics that ought to be here in the museums of Mexico instead of Philadelphia."

"And all for a profit," said Fleur quietly. "Is that what you think?"

He looked across at her. "It's true, isn't it?"

"I'm not privy to Mr. Flaxendon's motives," she said in the same even tone, though her heart was pounding. "But I do believe a great many people will benefit from the exhibition."

He studied her for a long moment, his

fingers turning the stem of his glass, his eyes moving slowly over her face. Finally he said, "Could I see your drawings from this afternoon?"

Fleur wet her lips. "I'm afraid the room is too dark."

In answer he took a silver cigarette lighter from his pocket and lit a candle stuck in a bottle at the center of the table. "Well?" he said.

"We're having such a lovely time. Let's not spoil it."

"You're proud of your work, aren't you?"

"Well, yes, but –"

"Then let me have a look at it. Please."

Reluctantly Fleur brought forth the tablet, and held her breath as he slowly turned the pages. Startled, she watched a show of keen interest spread over his face. Was it possible she might win him over to support the exhibition after all?

"These are very fine," he said when he had come to the last page. His gaze settled warmly on her. "You're very talented."

Fleur felt her face grow hot with the unexpectedness of his praise. "The displays I saw today at the museum were exactly what I needed to coordinate my imagination with what you've shown us this past week."

He was quiet for a few minutes, studying the gleam of candlelight captured in the glass of tequila and lime juice he had scarcely tasted. "Tell me how this work will be used," he said at last.

Fleur sipped her own drink before answering. "Are you sure you want to know?"

A flicker of rueful amusement played at his mouth's corner. "I promise not to sulk or make a scene."

"Very well then." She took a deep breath. If what she had to say made him angry, he had asked for it. "Before I leave the Yucatán, I hope to have compiled half a dozen more sketchbooks containing fabric designs and the clothing which can be made from them, plus designs for beads, pins, earrings – all kinds of jewelry."

She warmed to her subject. "And another idea came to me just this afternoon." Her gray eyes glowed in the candlelight. "I'd like to do some bedspreads, drapery, and towel designs as well. I saw some marvelous heavy, but loosely woven cloth in some of the displays that would make up beautifully."

Matt regarded her flushed cheeks and sparkling eyes. "You'll present these plans to Flaxendon for approval?"

She nodded. "If he likes them, we'll go

into immediate production. In April when the exhibition opens there will be four modelings a day of the clothes and jewelry. The show can be done in excellent taste, Matt," she said eagerly, unaware that she had laid a slender hand on his blunt-fingered one toying with the candleholder. "There need be nothing crass or commercial about it."

He took her hand and studied its oval fingertips, his expression betraying nothing of what he thought. "The models?"

"Girls of Hispanic origin if we can find them." He was actually listening, she thought excitedly. "If not, I've sketched a great many faces I've seen here. With the proper makeup and haircuts, we can achieve the effect I want. I'm sure of it."

"What *is* the effect you want?" He released her hand and leaned back in his chair.

"Classic simplicity," she answered at once. "Styles that will blend so naturally with Rita and Eric's work and the artifacts that it will seem as if the people whose culture is on display are right there walking about the viewers."

She waited a moment, little prickles of excitement dancing on her spine. "Well? What do you think?"

99

He raised his dark eyes and closed the sketchbook. "I think our dinner has arrived."

The *mole poblana de guajolote*, a delicious blend of twenty ingredients enfolding breast of turkey, raised an enticing aroma when the waitress set it before them, and Fleur tried to suppress the disappointment Matt's evasiveness had caused. "Is there chocolate in this?" she said after a few bites.

Matt grinned. "You have keen taste buds. Do you like it?"

"It's heavenly," she answered, wishing Matt could have answered her question as forthrightly.

"Then let me serve you some more."

She lifted her plate obediently. The turkey was delicious, but the bitter aftertaste of disappointment persisted.

"Tell me," said Matt when they were riding through a scarlet twilight on their way back to the hacienda. "What do you hope to gain out of this venture with Flaxendon?"

"Gain?" Fleur tried to restrain the excitement engendered by his second broaching of the subject of the exhibition. "What do you mean? Money?"

"If money is the answer."

"Well, it isn't. Or at least not entirely."

"But it does play an important part?"

She sighed. "Well, it's true that I am financially responsible for my mother and sister, but –"

"Financially responsible?" He made no effort to mask his surprise. "How did that happen?"

For a moment Fleur thought of saying *Do you always ask so many questions?*, but she discarded that in favor of the truth. "I'm afraid my father was not a business success. To make matters worse, he eased his failures by drinking too much. The combination broke his health. He had a dry-cleaning business that he finally lost, and shortly afterward he died. I was fourteen."

Matt spoke quickly. "I'm sorry to have brought up a painful subject."

"It was all a long time ago," she replied quietly. "I've gotten used to living with it."

"I'd say your mother managed very well."

"She was wonderful," Fleur agreed. "She's a seamstress, but arthritis has forced her in the last year to give that up. My sister Barbara helps out, but she's just beginning college."

"So the family finances are pretty well up to you."

"We'll manage."

"Look here." He glanced across at her, his brow furrowed. "How much would they need to see them through – say for the next few years?"

"What?" Fleur blinked. "What do you mean?"

"How much money? Twenty thousand? Thirty? I could give it to you."

Fleur's lips parted, closed, and parted again. *"Give* it to me!"

"It could all be arranged quite properly," he said at once. "No obligations. All very legal."

Fleur stared in round-eyed wonder. "Why, you're serious!"

"Of course."

"But you can't . . . People don't go around giving huge sums of money to other people they don't even know."

"I know you."

Fleur's laugh caught in her throat. "In two weeks' time? You must be joking."

"I was never more serious." From the set of his rugged profile against the scarlet sky, Fleur saw this was true. "Money is not a problem with me."

"Well, it soon will be if word gets around you're giving it away!"

"Does that mean you'll take it?"

"Of course not!" At his crestfallen look she could not contain her laughter. "You certainly didn't believe for a minute that I would?"

His jaw tightened. "I hoped you would. It would have given me pleasure, and you could give up this foolishness of Flaxendon's and –"

"Foolishness!" His words obliterated everything except a fierce defensiveness that spread like lava within her. "After all I've told you this evening, you still think that way about the exhibition?"

He gave an amused laugh. "Well, I think the whole idea is rather farfetched, to say the least."

"But you've seen my sketches. You said you liked them."

"And I meant it. That's why you shouldn't be using your talent in such a cheap way. And if it weren't for needing the money, you wouldn't have to."

Defensiveness turned to fury. "There will be nothing *cheap* about the Flaxendon Exhibition! Before you made your ridiculous offer to underwrite my family, you asked me what I hope to get out of this 'venture,' as you call it. If you'd do me the courtesy, I'd like to tell you."

He turned a bleak look upon her, and then

without speaking returned his gaze to the road.

Undaunted, she went on. "I hope to discover new ways of using the talent that's been given to me. I hope the ways I discover will bring pleasure and enlightenment to as many people as possible." Her eyes flashed angrily as she fought to control her voice. "I hope to prove to myself that I'm a useful human being fulfilling the place in life for which I was created."

A loud silence followed her words. Then without looking at her, Matt said, "End of sermon?"

She turned her face toward the dark fields of hennequen and let the tears she could no longer hold back slide hotly down her cheeks.

Chapter Nine

Before dawn the wistful call of an unfamiliar night bird woke Fleur. For a time she lay motionless, aware that the anguish which had accompanied her to bed the night before still ached within her. If only she could pluck Matt Kirkpatrick from her heart and toss him like some menacing weed far beyond the perimeters of her life!

But he was deeply rooted there, she acknowledged sadly. His smoldering eyes, that mouth whose touch set fire to her, the broad shoulders and strong arms that had drawn her to him yesterday in the car . . .

She tossed restlessly, picking from the shadows beyond the glass door the outline of the fountain growing sharper with the approaching dawn. Why couldn't she think less of his attractions and more of his acid temper? Of his biting remarks, of his scorn for the things she held dear?

But when she arranged his faults beside those qualities which so disarmed her, her resolution turned to dust, and she longed for his embrace with a frightening intensity that caused all else to wilt before it.

She sat up and drew her knees to her breast. Today she *must* make a fresh start. She must accept the fact that to Matt Kirkpatrick she was of no more importance than Antonia the maid. And of far *less* than Rita Pittman! Fleur rested her forehead on her knees, wishing the pressure might blot the other woman's face from her memory, and the sound of her name forever from her ears.

That was foolishness of course.

For the next four or five months, and perhaps longer if the exhibition were a success, she must work with Rita Pittman, and could not allow anger and jealousy to interfere.

So! Today would mark a new beginning.

But first she must have a little time alone to steel herself, to reaffirm, whenever her determination flagged, that Matt Kirkpatrick was poison for her. She must forget his eyes, his mouth, his arms, forget how her heart pumped when he held her and how quick and erratically her breath came when his gaze touched her.

She swung her legs over the side of the bed and reached into the closet for a simple wraparound skirt and plain white shirt. First she would take the jeep and ride over to Lapaleta to early mass.

She brushed her hair briskly before the mirror, glad to see a semblance of color rising in her pale cheeks. From Lapaleta she would go on to Chichén Itzá for a day of sketching, delaying there until late evening when the dinner hour had passed. Then she could slip into her room again, unnoticed.

For her "cure" to succeed, she must guarantee herself at least twenty-four hours away from the sight of Matt and Rita Pittman and even Eric Spandell, though he had not figured in the distressing scene last night that had ended her unhappy ride home from Mérida.

Dressed, she slipped through the quiet hall and out through the cool morning air to the jeep Matt had left parked at the end of the walkway. With relief she noted he had left the keys as well, though if he had not, she would probably have found them on the entry table where he usually tossed them.

Sliding behind the wheel, she was uncomfortably reminded of the last miserable miles of her ride home the evening before. Almost immediately after the conclusion of her "sermon," as Matt termed her somewhat impassioned expression of her philosophy, she had begun to feel the prickings of ingratitude.

The man at the wheel was narrow-minded and biting, quick tempered and cruelly unjust, but still he had made an amazing offer straight from the heart. Financial security for Mom and Barb, and no strings attached!

Heading the jeep down the road toward Lapaleta, Fleur sighed. And what had she done in response to such generosity? Flung it back at him as a "ridiculous" gesture. Well, one thing was certain. She'd never win any medals for tact, or graciousness either.

Of course, no self-respecting woman could accept from a man she scarcely knew a sum such as he had offered, but to have turned it down so rudely! No wonder he had no patience with her lofty ideals and smug little declarations about her gifts to humanity. If she could not even respond kindly to one human being, what chance was there she would "enlighten" the masses? It was a wonder he hadn't laughed her right out of the jeep. Her face stung at the memory. She would have to find some way to apologize.

But not today.

And not until she was able to put into some kind of perspective the abominable manner in which *he* had reacted on their arrival back at the hacienda.

Rita Pittman had been waiting up with cocktails, and it was clear at once how angry she was by the way her seductive lips drew back with a catlike snarl in greeting. "You two made quite a day of it."

Determined not to give herself away, Fleur put on a smile. "It *was* quite a day."

Matt gave Fleur a cold stare and brushed past to throw himself down on the couch next to Rita. Laying his arm suggestively across its back, he said with a yawn, "It was entirely too long, and boring beyond belief."

Fleur could scarcely believe her ears and felt her face flood with color under Rita's delighted scrutiny.

Matt motioned toward Rita's drink. "Pour me one of those things, will you?" He laid a hand on her sleek thigh. "On second thought, pour me two."

Rita laughed, her anger dissolving in the triumphant look she shot Fleur. "If the day was as abysmal as Matt says," she drawled lazily, "perhaps you'd better have one, too."

"No, thank you," Fleur replied stiffly. "I'm going to bed."

"A splendid idea," said Matt. Then to Rita, "There's way too much light in here."

"Don't bother to get up." Fleur's stony voice came from the doorway. With an angry flip of the light switch, she plunged the room into a darkness relieved only by a small lamp glowing in a far corner.

"Ah, much better," she heard Matt murmur, and it was all she could do not to turn back and upend the cocktail shaker over the two heads so close together in the shadows.

For hours after she went to her room, Fleur could hear laughter supplemented by the sounds of music. Were they dancing? She tossed on the rumpled sheets, fighting an impulse to slip out into the patio to get a glimpse of what was happening in the living room.

But she knew what was happening.

Matt and Rita Pittman were getting drunk. Touching each other. Kissing.

Her face flamed on the pillow. She was reminded again of Eric's photo of them locked together in the Dzibilchaltun under-brush, and for the second time that night hot tears covered her cheeks.

She must have drifted off to sleep soon afterward, for sometime later she found herself starting up, aware of muffled giggles in the hallway, and the sound of someone stumbling, then a door closing.

She waited tensely for Matt's return. Minutes passed. A cold fear clutched at her throat. Was he staying with Rita?

Something crumpled inside her. Only hours ago he had taken Fleur herself into his arms, explored her mouth with urgency, run his strong brown hands over her body. And now he was with Rita!

Stifling a cry, she buried her face in the pillow. She must get away from here, find some other job. But what kind of job? Where? She scarcely had enough money for the plane back to New York, much less

110

anything left over for Barbara and her mother. She was stuck here. Every day she must sit down at the table and look across at Matt Kirkpatrick's wide shoulders, his dark mane, and mocking eyes. Every day she must pass him in the hallway, listen to his voice, turn her eyes away from his mouth.

But not today, thank heavens!

Fleur caught sight of the outline of the church steeple at Lapaleta as the first rays of morning sun fell across the road. Today belonged to her, to marshal her inner resources, to gird herself with new determination.

Probably she should be grateful for this anguish. On her first job she was being forced to meet grueling personal challenges as well as those of her career. When she finally emerged from them triumphant, she would be forged in strength, equal to any task the future might hold.

But today... Today she must bind her wounds.

Turning into a narrow street of the sleepy little pueblo, she parked the jeep beside a massive adobe church. Old women in black shawls and younger ones wearing beribboned straw hats and cotton ponchos were streaming through its yawning entrance. Drowsy little boys stumbled across the

111

courtyard, their belted *chamarras* flopping in the dawn like bat wings.

Fleur slipped in among the worshippers and found a seat far to the left in the shadow of a statue painted in vivid colors, natural enough when regarded in the light of the sun-baked Mexican days, but somehow startling here in the early morning.

Bowing her head, she let the words of the soft-spoken priest wash over her. She understood nothing of what he said, but his tone eased her, and she concentrated on a word from her own language.

Forgive.

Forgive herself, for anger, for haughtiness and ingratitude in the face of Matt Kirkpatrick's kindness...forgive Matt Kirkpatrick for scoffing at her dreams, for his humiliation of her in front of Rita Pittman, for making her love him.

Fleurs eyes flew open. *Did she love him?*

Her heart beat unevenly. Certainly he reigned foremost in her thoughts, waking and sleeping. But love? *No.*

What she felt was infatuation. He overwhelmed her with his wealth, his offer to share that wealth with her family. She responded to him physically.

Fleur wet her dry lips, trying desperately not to think of his hard body pressed against

112

her own, of his hands at her waist. She felt drawn to him as a moth to a candle. Desire, yes. But love it was not.

At once she felt better. Absolved.

The mass was ending. She stood shakily, bathed in a warm glow of relief. Coming here had been an excellent idea. She had drawn strength and balance in this holy place. Confidently she moved out into the pale sunshine flooding the courtyard. Now for Chichén and a good day's work. She laid a hand on the door of the jeep and froze.

Parked next to it was the white Cadillac, and leaning against the front fender, arms folded, his dark eyes sweeping over her, was Matt. "Good morning."

Fleur's throat constricted. "Good morning."

"You're up early."

"So are you." Fleur opened the door of the jeep and slid under the wheel.

"I've been up all night."

"Oh?" Did he think she was fool enough to believe that when her own room was right next door to Rita's?

"Ramon's brother was injured in an accident just before midnight. I came over with him to see what we could do, but unfortunately there was nothing. He died about an hour ago."

Fleur stared. He couldn't be making this up. "I'm sorry."

"So am I. Ramon is in seeing the priest now."

Fleur glanced back at the church. "Is there anything I can do?"

"You could give me a ride back to the hacienda. I'd like to leave the car for Ramon."

Fleur's surprised gaze swept the sleek lines of the expensive automobile. Matt followed her glance. "It's the best thing I can do for him. He'll cut a fine figure with his relatives," he added gently. "Small comfort perhaps, but comfort nevertheless."

Fleur recalled the pride Ramon took in caring for the Cadillac and reflected that in Lapaleta where a man was rich if he owned a horse and cart, possession of a Cadillac, even for only a day, would indeed carry with it a comforting prestige. A swift look of appreciation replaced the hostility in her gray eyes. At least he cared how his servants felt.

"I'd be happy to share the jeep," she said evenly, "but I'm not going back to the house."

A look of disappointment as fleeting as had been her own of admiration clouded his black eyes. "I see. Well, never mind. Ramon can drive me home and bring the car back."

114

Ramon emerged at that moment from the church, a weeping woman on each arm, and the priest at his side. Fleur watched while Matt crossed the yard and spoke quietly to the bereaved women. Her heart twisted. How gentle he could be!

Quickly she left the jeep and crossed to where the group stood. "I'm so sorry to hear the sad news of your brother, Ramon." She nodded sympathetically at the women. "Don't trouble Ramon," she told Matt. "I can easily go back by way of the hacienda."

Matt spoke a few words in Spanish to Ramon and then took Fleur's elbow. Crossing the courtyard back toward the jeep, he said, "I appreciate your offer. I hope the change won't interfere with your work."

"It's quite all right." Fleur swung behind the wheel. "I was only going over to Chichén to sketch. I'll still have plenty of time."

Perhaps things had worked out for the best after all, she reflected, backing the jeep out of the churchyard. All day she would have had to hold at bay her next meeting with Matt. Now she could relax with that meeting behind her and concentrate completely on her work.

They drove in silence for a few miles, Matt whistling tunelessly. Finally he cleared his throat and spoke. "I wonder... Would you like to take a look at the gulf? And the Caribbean too, actually."

Fleur shot him a suspicious look. "What do you mean?"

"Well, I was just thinking. Progreso is only a few miles up ahead. Have you ever thought of going there?"

"I'm going to Chichén," she said firmly.

"I know, but this is Sunday."

She stared coldly across at him. "Really?"

He grinned. "What I mean is, the fishing boats are in at Progreso. They're quite a sight."

"Progreso." Fleur turned the word in her mouth. "That's the beach where the shells are so beautiful, isn't it?"

"The best place for shelling anywhere," he answered eagerly. "How about it?"

She frowned. "How about what?"

"Our going there. Today. Now."

"I'm taking you home!"

"You don't have to."

She was acutely aware that he had moved closer and that his arm lay just behind her head on the edge of the seat. "I want the day for myself."

"And I want to be with you." Without

116

warning, she felt his lips against her cheek. The jeep swerved.

"Stop it!" she cried. "You'll cause an accident!"

Obediently he moved back across the seat. "Just keep on going until you come to a fork and take a left."

She scowled. "That isn't the way to the hacienda."

If she had glanced across at him she would have seen the corners of his mouth turn up. "No, it isn't. It isn't the way to Chichén either."

She pulled off to the side of the road and stopped the jeep. "Look here. For Ramon's sake I agreed to take you back to the hacienda. I did not agree to let you spoil my day."

He blinked innocently. "Going to Progreso would do that?"

"Going with you would!"

"Oh." He sat back and folded his arms. "May I ask why?"

She gripped the steering wheel. "Because you're boring." Her face reddened. "Boring, boring, boring!"

His eyebrows lifted. He nodded understandingly. "It might be a long day."

"It might indeed!"

"But you wouldn't have to spend it with

me. I could sit on the porch. Smoke a few cigars. You could shell, swim if you like, tour the town. I'd just go along for the ride, show you how to get there."

"What porch?"

He lifted his brows. "Pardon?"

She drew her mouth into a tight little line. "You said you'd sit on the porch."

"The porch of my house there. Just a little cottage on the beach. I'd fix lunch. Take a nap. I wouldn't bother you in the least."

"I expect you have a hangover," she snapped.

He suppressed a grin. "A terrible one."

"You deserve it!"

"Let's talk about it while we're riding, shall we?"

She wanted very much to gather some shells for sketches she had in mind. But a whole day with Matt Kirkpatrick after yesterday? Could she bear it?

A little whisper nagged at the edge of her brain. Challenge. That was what this was all about, remember? Endurance. Proving herself fit for anything that turned up. Gritting her teeth, she started the motor. "A left, did you say?"

Chapter Ten

"This is what you call a cottage?" Fleur's astonished gaze swept the wide, screened gallery which wrapped the rambling cedar dwelling crouched on the shore. Coco palms waved lazily above its roof and bright red bougainvillea climbed the bannisters.

Beyond it, the blue Caribbean and the Gulf of Mexico joined waters to nibble at a white sand beach.

Matt folded his arms and let his eyes wander over the contours of the house as if he had never seen it before, then back to her. "What do *you* call a cottage?"

"Three or four rooms. Certainly not a place this size." She got down from the jeep and shaded her eyes from the sun. "Do you come here often?"

Matt leaned beside her on the jeep's fender. "Not often enough. My mother left it to me. For a while it depressed me to come here, but now..." He left the sentence dangling in the soft sea breeze.

Fleur surveyed his slumped shoulders, the tired tilt of his head. Normally he tended toward the hyperactive, all precision and drive, as if he were a machine set to operate only at top speed. But then, he had not slept all night. Or so he said.

She lifted a string bag from the seat. "Shall we take the food in?"

Half an hour ago when they had arrived on the outskirts of Progreso after a bumpy ride broken only occasionally by brief comments from Matt and equally brief answers from Fleur, Matt had directed her down an unpaved, narrow street to the only store that seemed open for business.

Inside, they had found on its dark shelves and in an antiquated icebox at the rear, luncheon supplies, milk, several kinds of fresh fruits and a beautiful silver-sided fish the proprietor assured Matt had been caught only an hour before.

"I hope you don't think I'm going to cook that," Fleur said when they were outside again. "Because if you do, then you might as well take it back."

Matt eyed the tail of the fish poking from the newspaper wrapped around its middle. "You might find it fun."

She lifted her nose delicately. "I've never cooked a fish in my life. I haven't the faintest idea how to get the head off, or the scales or anything else."

120

Matt grinned. "What else is there?"

"The tail, for one thing," Fleur answered with irritation. "Anyway, if you remember, your part of the bargain included fixing lunch."

"I remember." Matt opened the jeep door for her and swung himself over the other side, laying the fish between them to stare glassy-eyed at Fleur's trim ankle.

The narrow little streets were hardly more than alleyways, and Fleur's complete attention was required to maneuver the jeep successfully around family groups carrying fishing equipment toward a long pier jutting far out into the port waters.

Passing the harbor, Matt pointed out hundreds of tiny fishing vessels. "We'll come back later and look at those."

Fleur considered reminding him that the other part of the bargain was to leave her alone to do as she pleased, but the quaint little village had cast such a pleasant spell over her, she kept her peace rather than chance a fresh argument.

Then after a sharp turn and a short drive down a narrow, sandy lane, they came suddenly upon what Matt had termed the cottage, situated invitingly on a little knoll with the whole of the Caribbean stretched before it like a blue mirror. Fleur forgot everything else except the warm welcome its weathered hominess extended.

Matt took a key from his pocket and unlocked the front door. Inside, the same blanched cedar as the exterior comprised the flooring of large uncluttered rooms that opened one into another, creating a relaxing effect of spaciousness broken only by woven rugs scattered at intervals and some carefully selected pieces of clean-lined furniture finished in natural color.

"Zapote again?" Fleur ran her hand appreciatively over the hard, smooth wood.

Matt nodded and went into the kitchen with the groceries. "Remind me to make a call when we get back to the hacienda. I want you to have some samples to use for your beads."

Fleur blinked in astonishment. "That's very thoughtful." Especially since he abhorred the idea of the beads and everything else to do with the fashion show! She studied the back of his broad shoulders as he moved about the kitchen. He could be so nice, so accommodating when he wanted to. She turned away. And so obnoxious when he didn't.

Wandering to the windows, she looked out over the open expanse of water. "I'm going down and have a look at the shells."

He came to the door. "Sorry. I had my head in the pantry. What did you say?"

Her heart lurched at the sight of his muscular leanness framed in the doorway. If only his eyes did not caress her so! "I'm going to the beach."

She half expected him to say he would come along. Half wanted him to, she realized with a pang. But he only nodded and turned back toward the kitchen. "Take your time," he called. "There's no hurry about lunch. No hurry about anything."

So he wasn't coming after all?

Annoyed at her disappointment, she took the boardwalk through the white sand toward the beckoning waves which she scarcely saw. *Don't forget,* she told herself sternly. *He spent the night with Rita Pittman.*

But did he?

She remembered his tired eyes when he had spoken to her outside the church at Lapaleta. Had he really been with Ramon and his family instead? Was it possible she was mistaken in thinking she heard him entering Rita's room? Had she dozed and missed hearing him leave again? He could have let himself out the patio door.

But why would he do that when he had so obviously been inviting Rita to some sort of

123

tryst? They were drunk. With a girl like Rita, intimacy was almost certain to follow.

Fleur swallowed a lump in her throat. What would it be like to lie very close to that broad chest, those lean thighs? To give oneself without reservation to his hard embrace?

She brought herself up sharply. She had no intention of ever finding out, so why was she torturing herself? She stepped off the boardwalk into the soft white sand and halted.

At her feet lay an assortment of the most perfect angel wings she had ever seen, even in the finest shell shop in New York where she often wandered between classes. Beyond, half a dozen baby's bonnets nestled in the sand. Augur shells and banded tulips were scattered everywhere, and delicate pen shells, scallops, and coral dotted the shore.

Forgetting everything except this astonishing treasure flung from the sea, she caught up the hem of her skirt, fashioning a kind of hammock for the bounty, too excited to mind the damp sand within the cloth or the grit beneath her fingernails. Delightedly she darted from shell to shell, pausing only long enough to hold a special beauty up to the light, then dashing on to another.

All at once she was aware that she was not

alone, and whirling, saw Matt standing at the end of the boardwalk, a peculiar smile upon his lips and a reed basket in one hand. "I thought you'd need this." His eyes moved over the smooth white skin of her thighs, exposed by the skirt lifted to hold her treasure. "I see you do."

Bright spots of color sprang up in her cheeks. She could not drop the hem and hold the shells too, so she stood her ground while Matt drew near. When the rough reed brushed her legs, she spilled her gleanings carefully into the basket and shook the sand from her skirt.

He was close enough that her fingertips met his, clutching the edge of the basket, and she felt an electrifying thrill sweep up her loins. Would she never grow used to that magnetism that leaped from his skin to hers whenever they touched?

She drew away. "The sea is beautiful."

When he did not speak, she turned to find him staring at her. Her lips parted. If he should kiss her now, there was not a chance she could resist him. Her legs were like water, and the whole of the ocean pounded in her eardrums.

"Will you take this, or shall I set it down?"

He was holding out the basket.

"Oh." Mechanically she reached for it, aware that this time he turned the handle so their fingers would not meet again.

"Enjoy yourself."

Stunned, she watched him stride up off the boardwalk. The nerve of him! Deliberately enticing her, then turning away. Well, who needed him? If he couldn't at least spend a few minutes with her on the beach, then let the devil take him!

Smarting at his dismissal of her, she started off across the sand, realizing too late that her angry footsteps had smashed dozens of fragile shells. Dropping in a dejected heap, she buried her face in her hands, as powerless as she had been last night to halt the flow of stinging tears that slid down her cheeks.

Gradually, however, the pulsations of the waves soothed her, and after an hour and a half of quiet meditation during which she reviewed her resolutions of the night before, Fleur collected a few more specimens in the reed basket and made her way back to the cottage.

As she drew near, her nostrils caught a tantalizing aroma, and she saw a thin wisp of smoke rising from somewhere toward the back of the house.

Following a path lined with purple sand

verbena, she came around a corner and discovered Matt dozing in the sun beside a barbecue pit where the silver fish now gleamed a golden brown on the spit.

At her step, Matt started up guiltily. "Just nodded off for a moment."

But he appeared so refreshed, Fleur was certain he had slept much longer, and a sudden rush of tenderness came unbidden at the sight of his flushed face and heavy-lidded eyes. "Why don't you rest awhile longer, and I'll go and make a salad."

"Everything's done," he said with a yawn. "I knew as soon as I was still I'd fall asleep, so I tended to all the luncheon details first."

Entering the house, Fleur saw he had set up an attractive table by a large window looking out over the water, and a crisp salad filled a wooden bowl in the table's center. Beside bright placemats laid with silver forks, stood tall glasses waiting for milk. In a moment Matt came in bearing the fish on a wooden platter.

Fleur had never tasted barbecued fish before, and she let the tender flakes melt on her tongue while her eyes sparkled with admiration. "You're quite a cook, Dr. Kirkpatrick." She leaned back with a sigh, swallowing the last of a delectable little tidbit

127

called *pan dulce*. "You could give Josie a run for her money."

He smiled absently. "You enjoyed the beach?"

"Very much. The air's so fresh here, so relaxing. No wonder you fell asleep."

A flinty gleam appeared in his black eyes. "The hangover had something to do with that, too." When she said nothing, he went on. "I drank too much because I was angry at you."

Fleur stiffened, unable to stem a tide of irritation his words had loosed. "How childish!"

"It is, isn't it." With a sigh, he rubbed the back of his neck. "I wish I'd thought of that last night."

"You seemed to be preparing to enjoy yourself. Perhaps it was worth it."

His eyes watched her slender fingers moving nervously on the fringe of the yellow table mat. "Did we disturb you?"

"I was disgusted." The haughtiness of her tone annoyed even her. "But I suppose men must have flings from time to time."

He repeated her words thoughtfully. "A fling. Is that what it was?"

"How should I know?" Why did he have to bring this up just as she was beginning to enjoy herself? Could there never be any peace with this man?

He got up. "Let's go in the living room. I want to talk."

"What about this?" Fleur glanced at the dishes on the table and back at the untidy kitchen. "Shouldn't we clean up first?"

He pulled back her chair. "On the way out, I'll stop at Rosita's and leave the key. She'll come back later and tend to everything."

How nice to have servants at one's beck and call, thought Fleur, following him into the living room. There, to her surprise, she caught sight of her open sketchbook on the couch beside a stack of reference books. He followed her glance. "I've been looking at those again."

"My sketches?"

He nodded. "I was trying to understand what they mean to you."

His words had a curious effect on Fleur. He had not closed his mind to her work after all! And perhaps not to her either. She felt a surge of joy. "And what do you think?"

"They're excellent, of course. I've told you that." He sat down across from her, his muscular frame filling up the graceful chair. "I can see how your designs would be important."

129

She held her breath as he went on. "I'm glad if Flaxendon had to incorporate business and the Mayan artifacts, you were the artist he chose."

Artist. The word poured over her like precious balm. "Then..." She hesitated. "Then you feel more satisfied that the exhibition won't be a betrayal of the Mayan culture?"

His frank gaze met her gray eyes. "I'm trying to feel that way."

"Why?" The question escaped her lips without warning, and she drew a sharp breath. How could she be so stupid as to alienate him just as he was making headway toward a sensible viewpoint?

But his answer surprised her. "Because it's the way *you* feel."

She could scarcely breathe. "Does that matter?"

"More than I realized." His eyes burned into hers. "When I saw you down at the beach earlier, your hair blowing, your skirt tucked up to hold the shells – no, no, don't be embarrassed. You were lovely." His gaze moved over her, touching every part of her. "But more than lovely; there's a sense of wonder about you. And a . . . a contentment." His voice grew hollow. "I've never felt that."

130

"I wonder why," she said softly, moved by his surprising admission. "You live in a beautiful land surrounded by every kind of wonderful thing. You have the means to share whatever you choose –"

"Share," he broke in, deep in thought. "That's your theme, isn't it."

"Perhaps it's yours too," she said swiftly. "Whenever you speak of Mexico or the Yucatán, whenever I've watched your eyes light up when you showed us the ruins, I've seen a man completely absorbed, wholly alive. Sharing."

He said nothing, his eyes on her.

"On the way to Mérida," she went on with increasing eagerness, "you were speaking about the terrain and the windmills. I wish you could have seen your face! But then –" She broke off.

"Yes?"

She took a breath. "Then you remembered your bitterness, you remembered to feel sorry for yourself."

"Sorry for myself!"

"You have everything a man could want, and yet you're full of anger so much of the time."

"You talk of sharing," he shot back. "Why didn't you let me share my money instead of rejecting my offer as ridiculous?"

Her own words coming from his mouth rang harshly in Fleur's ears. "The word was ill chosen. Your offer wasn't in the least ridiculous." She leaned forward, eyes bright, chin trembling. "It was beautiful and generous and overwhelming. I apologize for my insensitivity."

He was silent, looking at her. "I apologize too," he said finally.

"For what?"

"For having labelled your philosophy a sermon." A ghost of a smile played at the corner of his mouth. "Though perhaps you will admit it was a bit preachy."

She smiled in spite of herself. "And of course you don't appreciate being preached at. Who does? Still..." She sighed. "That happens to be the way I feel. I want to give to life because so much has been given to me."

"An unsuccessful father. A dependent mother. You think you have been dealt with generously?"

"Love has been given me." Her voice hung softly in the quiet room. "Heaped upon and running over. We didn't have wealth, but we found joy in each other. Except for my father, it was enough for all of us." Her eyes glowed. "You can have the kind of joy we knew, Matt."

"Can I?" His jaw hardened. "Before he died, I hated my father."

"For marrying Mrs. Flaxendon?"

"For degrading the memory of my mother by marrying Mrs. Flaxendon," he corrected acidly.

"But your mother was dead, Matt." Fleur spoke gently. "Perhaps he was lonely, as you are now. Can you blame him for wanting to find happiness?"

Matt got to his feet abruptly. "How did we get into this?"

Fleur blinked. "You invited me to discuss it with you."

"Then consider the discussion closed." All trace of warmth had left his voice. "It's after four. We ought to start back.

A dull ache that had begun near Fleur's heart spread throughout her body. From a tight throat she said, "I'm ready any time." She picked up her sketchbook from the couch. "What about these books. Do you want to leave them for Rosita too?"

He had gone to stare out at the sea, but at her question he turned. The tautness at his mouth eased. "I got them out for you. I thought they might help with your designs."

"Oh, Matt." All her reserves began to crumble like sand fortresses. "Why do we always quarrel and hurt each other? Why can't we make each other happy – if only for a little while?"

His lips parted. He drew a breath. "Could I ever make you happy?"

Her answer came out a whisper. "I think so."

Then they were in each other's arms, his lips searching hungrily for hers, her body pressed to his.

"Fleur, Fleur."

She felt his warm breath in her hair, her mouth moving over his stubbled cheek.

"You'll scratch your face," he mumbled hoarsely. "It's been hours since I shaved."

"I don't care."

They sank together on the couch, his lips closing over hers, and she felt the hard thrust of his chest against her breasts. Time stopped, and she was lost in the ecstasy of his mouth turning hotly upon her own, locked against the strength of him, yielding to the pressure of his thighs, his hunger.

Trembling, she pulled away. His grip tightened. "Be mine, Fleur."

"No, Matt, no." She buried her face in his neck. "We'd only be resolving the moment, compounding your misery."

"Don't be foolish."

She let his lips move over her throat,

fighting the longing to give herself to him. "Trust me, Matt," she said finally, easing herself from his arms. "For now, let's hold fast to what we've found, not grasp for something we aren't ready for."

'We are ready!'

"Only physically. I'd need to know your heart first – and you mine, for us to be happy, to know contentment."

He regarded her for a long moment while her hopes sank. Had she lost him again? This time forever?

Then he placed his hand on her neck and drew her to him. "All right," he murmured. "You're the happiness expert. I'll listen – for a little while, but at least let me hold you."

With a sob of relief she nestled close into his arms.

Chapter Eleven

On the drive back to the hacienda they spoke mostly of inconsequential things. His years at the university in Dublin, childhood memories, her experiences at design school. But Fleur's slender hand lay on the seat between them, and more than once his square brown one covered it, giving a reassuring squeeze.

Fleur basked in a warm glow of contentment. Not since she had come to the Yucatán had she felt such peace, such a sense of rightness at being here. She had not known Matt until this afternoon. She had seen only a handsome, demanding male of enormous attraction, not the complex, searching person he actually was.

It was in bouts of uncertainty that he became his most caustic, she saw now. He struck out at what he wanted but could not draw into his own life. Only in the safe harbor of his professional competence did he move with true assurance and calm.

She closed her eyes for a moment. What a sweet task it would be to stay close to his side as he discovered himself. What a joy to know that less and less frequently would he need to turn angrily upon others in order to safeguard his vulnerability.

"Tired?"

Her lids lifted, and she focused her soft gray eyes on his mouth, curved now in tender regard. "A little. But in the nicest way imaginable. Thank you for taking me to Progreso."

He put his arm about her shoulders and

pulled her to him. "Perhaps we can go back again while you're here."

An awareness that a time was fast approaching when she would not be here occurred to them both at once, and their eyes met.

Matt spoke first. "Maybe I'll come to Philadelphia for the exhibition."

"Oh, Matt! Will you?" Fleur's eyes shone. "Then you could see for yourself how right the whole idea is."

His arm tightened on her shoulder. "I could see you. I'm more interested in that."

They were silent while each one thought of the months to be lived through between Fleur's departure and the opening of the exhibition. "Will you stay in Philadelphia until April or go back to New York?" Matt asked after a while.

"It depends, I suppose, on how the work goes. I'm free to devote all my time as long as it's needed."

"What about Christmas? Will you go home then?"

"Oh, yes." She smiled. "Mom and Barb and I always share that season."

"Share. There's that word again."

Fleur spoke quickly to blot out the bleakness of his tone. "Why not share it with us?"

He took his eyes from the road for a second to regard her intently. "Come to New York?"

"Why not?" Her smile dimmed. "Or perhaps you've made other plans."

"I usually go to Mexico City. I have friends there."

"I see." What she saw was a festive whirl of parties and crowds of exciting people contrasting starkly with a memory of her mother's simple apartment, the useful gifts the three of them exchanged. "Then I'm afraid you'd be terribly bored with New York at least with *my* neighborhood."

"Are you withdrawing your invitation?"

"Of course not, but I don't think you'd find the Yule season in the Normandy household anything like what you're accustomed to."

"That settles it then!" He flashed a brilliant smile. "Look for me on the twenty-fourth."

He was serious! Fleur thought she might float right out of the jeep. Wait until Mom and Barb hear! They'll have to start cooking right away. Cookies, candy, fruit-cake. Her eyes danced. "Have you ever tasted pfeffernüsse? Or debkuchen? Do you hang up a stocking?"

Matt laughed. "I haven't and I don't." He

gave her shoulder a squeeze. "But in New York, I have a feeling I'll be doing both."

When the hacienda came into sight, Fleur moved over toward the window. At Matt's quizzical glance, she said, "I still think romantic entanglements will complicate our work – especially if they're observed."

Matt acknowledged this reference to the first time he had kissed her by grinning broadly. "You mean Rita?"

At the name, Fleur felt a little cloud pass over her happiness. "And Eric, too," she said quietly. "What do you think of him?"

"Personally he strikes me as a rather sour individual, but I do admire his work."

I think he's a person who seldom gets the breaks." Fleur's brow furrowed. "I think his pessimism wards them off, rather like the way citronella offends the *garrapatas*."

Matt laughed. "What a funny little thing you are. Always analyzing people."

Fleur blinked. "Am I really?" She was quiet for a moment. "That must make others uncomfortable."

Matt shot her a wry grin. "When the analysis is unflattering, I can testify that it does indeed!"

She realized there was an element of humor in his comment, but the truth stung.

139

They had come to a stop at the front door, precluding further discussion. Matt reached across and squeezed her hand once more, smiling reassuringly, but Fleur could not quite shake off the feeling of apprehension his remark had stirred, and she made a mental note to think more about her own faults and less about those of others.

Dinner was a pleasant affair. Rita seemed unusually affable, much to Fleur's relief, for she had dreaded seeing her after last night's debacle, particularly since she, Fleur, had spent the whole day with Matt.

The svelte archaeologist seemed not the least interested in where they had been, however, and spoke mainly of the productivity of her own day. "Eric and I accomplished quite a lot this afternoon," she said smugly. "I think we'll be ready for Uxmal by Wednesday."

Eric made no comment, but attended strictly to the delicious shrimps in green sauce Josie had prepared, and to Fleur's way of thinking, he seemed rather subdued.

As soon as dinner was over, Matt excused himself to drive over to Lapaleta for the rosary of Ramon's brother; Rita, with the comment that she had never spent much time in the quaint little market town, asked if she might come along.

Spandell shot an inquiring look in Fleur's direction and seemed bemused when it was met with a calm gaze in return.

Fleur was not at all perturbed that Rita sought Matt's company for the evening. She was glad, in fact. If Rita felt secure in Matt's attention – which Fleur was now sure would mean nothing beyond an effort to be courteous – then that was a safety valve for all of them. Nothing would get done if Rita continued as angry as she had been last night, and now that Matt seemed to approve of the project, Fleur was more desirous than ever that it go smoothly.

For more than an hour after Matt and Rita departed for Lapaleta, Fleur, cozily ensconced on the couch in the living room, absorbed herself in the books Matt had given her that afternoon. She found in their pages an interesting background for many of the objects she had seen in the museum at Mérida, and from the information, her own ideas expanded, though she did find her powers of concentration not quite equal to her memories of the afternoon.

She was entertaining the idea of having a glass of wine and going to bed, when Eric came into the living room. He was dressed casually in the chinos he wore at work and an open-throated shirt of a light material that revealed his slight but well-proportioned build.

He sat down on the couch beside her with a sigh. "What are those?" He flipped the cover of a book idly. "More references?"

Fleur stretched, stifling a yawn. "Matt had them at his house in Progreso. They're fascinating."

Spandell flipped several more pages, but it was obvious he was more interested in pursuing the details of her day than the history of Mayan artifacts. "Had yourself quite a time down there, I suppose."

Fleur tried to shake off the annoyance his tone aroused. "It was a lovely day. The Caribbean is beautiful. But you're well acquainted with that, of course."

"Not with Progreso. It's off the beaten track."

"That's one of its charms, I think. It's still a sleepy little village. I hope it stays that way."

"What's Matt's cottage like?"

"Big. Simple." Fleur warmed at her memory of the steadfast house by the sea. If she could live anywhere in the world, she thought, she might very well choose there. "Matt cooked."

Eric's sardonic grin twisted his face. "Matt's being quite attentive. This is two days in a row."

"He had business in Mérida," Fleur said warily.

The grin widened. "Monkey business?"

"Really, Eric. If you came in here to annoy me, you're succeeding nicely."

"If you want to see someone *really* annoyed, you should have spent yesterday at Chichén with Rita," he answered grimly.

"I don't think she had cause for annoyance," Fleur said in a crisp tone. "She planned to go to Chichén, and that's where she went."

"Her plan included Matt."

"Why should she consider it his duty to be at her beck and call?" Fleur said with growing irritation. "He's given us more time than he bargained for already."

Eric raised his hands to ward off her sharp reply "I'm only telling you the way it was."

Fleur softened. "Did she give you a bad time?"

"Not as bad as today." He sighed. "She didn't get up until after lunch. When she discovered you two were gone again, she got deadly."

Fleur felt a shiver of apprehension. "What do you mean?"

"I warned you she can be ruthless when she's after a man."

"And you think she's after Matt?"

His cold laughter startled Fleur. "Are you kidding? If you can't see that, you must be blind."

"I know she's flirting with him." Fleur shifted uneasily, remembering the scene last night in the living room. "Anyway, it seems to me she's spent as much time with him as anyone."

"You're thinking of last night." At Fleur's surprised glance, he went on. "I came in from a swim a little before midnight. They were still at it."

As Eric painted unpleasant pictures with his words, all the lovely glow left over from her day at Progreso sifted away like quicksand.

"She was really getting ready to tie one on."

Getting ready? And Eric had said "she." What about Matt? "Did you join them?"

His lip curled. "I wasn't going to. I know Madame Pittman. I didn't want any more busted cameras, but Matt insisted. He was sober as a judge and looked pretty sick of the whole thing to me."

Then he didn't have a hangover. Fleur

frowned. Why had he said so? To keep his hard line image intact?

"Before I could decide whether to or not, the news came about Ramon's brother, and Matt left."

"And you stayed?"

Eric suddenly looked uncomfortable. "For a while," he mumbled. Fleur looked sharply at him. Was it possible *he* spent the night in Rita's room? He said he hated her, but did he? They had been lovers once. Or at least Spandell had made it known that Rita desired him, and he had thrown her over. Perhaps if the truth were known, it was the other way around.

Fleur felt smothered all at once, stifled by the vindictive intrigue that seemed always to surround Rita, and Eric also. She wished Matt would return so that the reassuring sight of his face might ease the peculiar tension within her.

"But Rita seemed in such a good mood at dinner," she said, unsure whether she was trying to comfort herself or to test the truth of Spandell's earlier statement that Rita had turned deadly when she discovered Fleur and Matt were away together.

Eric nodded gloomily. "That's a bad sign, that sugary sweetness. She raged all afternoon about you."

"She said you and she accomplished a lot of work."

"At least that part's true. She's at her best when the adrenaline is flowing full stream." His expression changed abruptly. "Watch out for her, Fleur. She'll get you if she can."

"Get me?" Fleur suppressed a shudder. "Aren't you being rather melodramatic?"

"Oh, I don't mean physically harm you. Though she might enjoy that too."

"What *do* you mean, then?"

He gave her a solemn look.

"She'll wreck your career if she can find a way."

"Oh, Eric!"

"I'm serious. She had a shot at mine. I know what I'm talking about."

"But if Flaxendon spared you, surely –"

"He'd do the same for you? Maybe." His small eyes fastened on her anxious face. "But it isn't Flaxendon she'll try to turn against you."

Fleur stared. "Who, then?"

His gaze was level. "Matt."

Chapter Twelve

Though Fleur waited up, purposely dawdling over the books in the living room long after Eric had gone to his room, Rita and Matt did not return. Finally, at a quarter past eleven, she turned out all the lights except one in the entryway and a small lamp in the living room and went to bed herself.

She was more disappointed than she liked to admit at not having seen Matt to say good night, but she made a determined effort to shrug off this new dependence on his presence. It would never do to become so absorbed in exploring her awakening feelings for him that she allowed thoughts of him to interfere with her work.

But that had already happened, she realized.

She sat down at the dressing table and stared reluctantly at her troubled face in the mirror. Only for a brief time tonight had she been able to really concentrate on the books he had given her. Of course Eric's gloomy visit hadn't helped, but even before Spandell came into the living room, she was listening for the sound of the jeep's motor and glancing at her watch.

With a sigh she slipped out of her clothes and went into the bathroom to draw a warm bath. Looking about she discovered there were no towels laid out, though Antonia, the little *mestizo* maid, was usually so meticulous in seeing that everything was exactly as it should be when she cleaned. This morning she, like me, thought Fleur ruefully, must have had something else on her mind besides her work.

Reaching into the linen closet, Fleur felt her fingers close around a small vial and drew it forth. Bath oil. Funny she'd never noticed it there before.

Unscrewing the lid, she poured a few drops into the steamy water and slid in herself. She closed her eyes, letting the fragrance slowly envelop her. Had Matt selected it, she wondered, or was it something left over from Mrs. Flaxendon's reign?

She sniffed. Sandalwood? No. The scent was heavier, more exotic. She sat up. Almost unpleasant in fact. Turning the tap, she let more water into the tub. The scent was nearly overpowering, but it made her skin feel marvelous.

Once more she slithered down into the

silken water and closed her eyes. *Matt.* She spoke the name inside her brain, reveling in the intimate tones it produced, in the suggestions that swirled like smoke when she thought of the man it represented. Was she being foolish to entertain the thought that he might care deeply for her? He was coming to her home for Christmas. That meant something, didn't it?

Or was Christmas for him simply a lonely time, despite the gay round of festivities in Mexico City? It might be that he longed for the warmth of a family circle, no matter whose family it was.

She let the water cover her shoulders. But she had seen his eyes. He *did* care for her. Why had he lied then about having had too much to drink?

With a sigh she sat up and began to soap her arms. She could linger here until her skin shriveled and never answer all the questions whirling in her mind. Besides, there was one more thing she must do tonight, and she was eager to get to it.

Toweling dry quickly, she slipped into a filmy yellow nightgown, noting how the scent of the bath oil followed her into the bedroom. She wrinkled her nose with displeasure. Only a drop or two had gone into

149

the tub, but even that little bit was too much! Opening the patio door a few inches, she stood for a moment breathing gratefully the fresh cool air and listening to the muted sound of the night.

Then, turning back to the dresser, she pulled the top drawer out and groped carefully among its contents. The Vera Cruz bowl Matt had lent her was there somewhere, wrapped with care in a silk scarf and embedded in her lingerie where it would be safe from bumps and knocks.

She wanted to examine it under a strong light. Before she went to sleep, she intended to memorize the special colorations of that glaze. Sometimes sleep imprinted impressions of that sort more thoroughly on the subconscious mind than daytime study. Then when the impressions came back in her own designs they always seemed keener, sharper, and more exciting.

Her fingers moved carefully through the soft folds of underclothing. When she found nothing, she pulled the drawer out all the way and set it on top of the dresser.

"All right. Where are you?" she chided. As if she were engaged in a game of hide-and-seek, she cautiously lifted out gowns and underpants, stacking them neatly beside the drawer until the brown wood of its bottom shone starkly in the lamplight.

No bowl.

Fleur swallowed a rising wave of panic. It was here. Somewhere.

She stared blankly into the barren interior of the drawer. Could she possibly have moved it to a safer place and forgotten about it?

Hardly. But it was not here, so she must have.

Fighting back an onrushing tide of alarm, she went quickly to the closet and rummaged through the contents of its side shelves. From there she returned on wobbly legs to the bathroom. A bottle of aspirin. Soaps. A jar of shampoo. *Where was the Vera Cruz glaze?*

Resisting an impulse to rush out to the curio cabinet to see if somehow Matt had replaced the bowl in its proper setting, she sank on the bed and tried to still her trembling hands. Matt had entrusted her with a treasure, and now she couldn't find it.

What could she tell him?

She wet her lips and concentrated with all her might on recalling the evening Matt had handed her the bowl. She had left the dining room, come straight to her bedroom, and –

of course! She had only *thought* of wrapping it in the silk scarf. Instead she must have tucked it into the case with her sketchbooks and the fabric swatches she had bought at the market in Lapaleta.

Hastily she dropped to her knees and drew forth the leather case from beneath the bed. It was locked. A chilling thought passed up her spine as she scrambled in her purse for the key. Wasn't it the other way around? Hadn't she first thought of the case, and discarded that idea in favor of the silk scarf in the drawer?

With icy fingers she fitted the key in the lock and lifted the lid, knowing even before she saw the flat folds of the fabric and the smooth stack of sketchbooks there was no bowl in the case.

Fleur's stomach turned over. She sank limply to the floor. *Think!* she commanded. There was no way the bowl could have gotten up and walked out of the room. It was here! And she must find it tonight.

Frantically her eyes flew over the room. Had she walked in her sleep and moved it from its hiding place? Had Antonia displaced it while cleaning?

For what seemed hours, she searched fruitlessly. In the midst of her efforts she heard the front door opening, light laughter

152

in the hallway. Rita and Matt were back, but she did not even glance at her watch to see how long they had been away. Everywhere she looked she expected to uncover the orange bowl, but it was not under or behind or inside anything.

The bowl had simply disappeared.

Wearily Fleur crawled into bed. For a time she lay staring up through the darkness toward the ceiling trying to reenact the evening Matt had given her the bowl. When she closed her eyes she could see it gleaming in the darkness, and her fingers ached to take it up and clutch it to her breasts. If only she could have it in her hands again! She'd never set it down until it was safely locked in the curio cabinet.

Toward morning she slept, but only fitfully, and when a tiny yellow bird began to sing in the patio at daybreak, she rose wearily and began her search again.

When neither Matt nor Rita appeared for breakfast, Fleur could scarcely hide her relief. After the morning search had unearthed nothing, she finally faced the fact that she must make some kind of explanation to Matt. The thought paralyzed her.

What was there to say? I'm sorry, but

somehow I've lost the priceless bowl you loaned me? Impossible!

Giving only superficial replies to Spandell's morning chatter, she gulped her breakfast coffee, and muttering something unintelligible, made away in the jeep shortly after seven.

So numb was she, she paid no attention to where she was going, but after a few miles saw she was on the road to Chichén Itzá and let the jeep have its way as she might a trusted horse, unable to think of anything except the panic which now wholly possessed her.

What a coward she was not to have stayed at the hacienda and faced Matt with the truth. But the long, sleepless night had left her distraught. Besides, there must be a perfectly obvious explanation for the disappearance of the bowl. She had simply been too shocked and alarmed to see it. Alone at Chichén she could collect her thoughts and the mystery would clear itself.

Comforted somewhat, she parked the jeep and approached El Castillo, awed as always by the majesty of the pyramid which dwarfed the jungle beyond. Sketchbook in hand, she crossed the beige softness of the damp grass and began the steep climb leading to the straight combless roof some seventy-five feet above her.

Ninety-two steps led up the side of the Temple of Kukulcan, she recalled dizzily, and she was thankful for the hand chain that aided her ascent. Then suddenly the azure sky switched places with the furred earth, and Fleur dropped to her knees, clutching the cold links with whitened fingertips. She must be out of her mind to be scaling the temple as tired as she was! Tremulously she glanced at the ground and then toward the flat top of El Castillo. Retreating would take longer now than finishing the climb.

Shakily she rose again, her mouth powder dry, her palms sweaty. Once she had gained the top, she reassured herself, she could rest as long as she liked. The vertigo would pass when her blood pressure stabilized.

Apparently her efforts to calm herself were successful, and after what seemed an eternity she at last attained the ninth terrace and sank, trembling, on the wide stones. Thank heavens it was too early for the tour buses coming out from Cancun and Mérida. She needed the place to herself.

Through the crystal morning, the causeway to the north was visible only as a narrow winding path that disappeared shortly into the jungle. Far below, the white columns of

155

the Temple of the Warriors shone in the sunlight. Wearily Fleur wondered if from that perspective she appeared as only another knob in the ornate carvings that surrounded her.

If only she *were* a knob! Or better still, invisible. What was she going to tell Matt? How could she bear the anger and disappointment her confession was certain to produce? How could she live with the knowledge of her carelessness?

But even while she reprimanded herself, common sense reasserted itself. She had not been careless. It was now as clear as the morning air that she had indeed meticulously wrapped the Vera Cruz glaze in the blue silk scarf and laid it with utmost caution among her lingerie. What had happened to it after that moment she could not say, but whatever it was, she had had nothing to do with it.

But if Matt reminded her that she was responsible for the bowl, that it was entrusted to her for safe-keeping . . .

Then she would remind *him* that she could not be expected to hover over it night and day, and he knew that when he gave it to her. Obviously one of the servants had discovered it and, aware of its value, been tempted and removed it.

Who? Antonia? The bright smiling face

of the serving girl flashed before Fleur. Or
Ramon perhaps? But he was in Lapaleta.
Anyway, he rarely came into the house. Josie
then? Fleur sighed. Never. A robber? Could
there have been burglars? Other things
might be missing and their absence not yet
discovered!

Fleur's heart lifted. That was the answer!
Everyone in the area was certainly aware that
Matt was a wealthy man. With everyone
gone all day and Josie stuck away in the
kitchen, anyone could have slipped into the
house.

Cheered, Fleur rose. As soon as she got
back, she would find a way to be alone with
Matt and tell him what had happened. A
remembrance of his arms about her in the
house at Progreso stole over her, and her
weariness slipped from her like a discarded
cloak. He was gentle, tender. He would
understand.

In the meantime, why should she waste
this glorious day?

Alone, she could peruse the ruins more
thoroughly than she so far had had the
opportunity to do. There would be time
enough to talk to Matt later.

Without a trace of her former
unsteadiness, she clambered along the steep
temple sides, pausing at will to observe the

tigers, serpents, coats of arms, and rosettes ancient hands had carved across the walls.

At the base of the pyramid she came upon an opening. Venturing inside, she climbed a dark, spiral stairway that opened into a tiny room so dimly lit that minutes passed before she was able to make out chunky legs supporting a throne, and in another moment, the head and tail of a jaguar surmounting it.

Was it Matt or Rita who had told her that it was the Red Jaguar who had driven the deer from the cornfields and thus become a god? Straining, she gazed in fascination at the small scarlet beast spotted with inlaid jade. Even its eyeballs were of the same green stone, and within its open jaws, razor-sharp incisor teeth of flint glinted in the veiled light.

An eerie feeling seized her. One could be too much alone in such a spot where hundreds of years before worshippers had lost their lives to appease Kukulcan. Beyond, in the cenote, maidens had been thrown screaming to their deaths, and babies, whose tears it was said were sweetest to the gods, had died too.

Shivering, she turned toward the stairway. But once again in the sunlight, she wondered what foolishness had possessed her back there in the inner chamber, and laughed a little at her own faintheartedness.

Another hour passed while Fleur wandered through the ruins, pausing finally beside an amusing stone Chacmool crouched in an excruciating position, its shell eyes staring, its hands outstretched for alms. She was sketching it when the sound of an approaching motor broke the quiet.

Standing, she discovered the pickup coming to a halt along the edge of the road. The door on the passenger side opened, and Eric Spandell climbed out, followed by Rita. In a moment, Matt came around from the other side.

Fleur caught her breath. From where they had stopped, the jeep was not visible. If she hurried around the temple, perhaps she could escape them.

Her feet were already moving rapidly across the stones when she halted herself. How stupid! She had already resolved the problem of the bowl. There was nothing to run from. But still she could not shake off a feeling of dread, and stood uncertainly until Matt appeared suddenly at the corner of an ancient wall a few feet away.

"Fleur!"

"Hello." Her heart turned over at the sight of his glad smile.

"So this is where you ran off to so early. Spandell said he hadn't the faintest idea what got into you, you were in such a rush at breakfast."

"I wanted to catch the light," she mumbled. He had come close to her, still smiling, but now he halted, a shadow crossing his face.

"What's wrong?" she said.

He hesitated uncertainly. "Your perfume."

Fleur almost laughed. "What?"

"That scent you're wearing. What is it?"

Rita and Spandell had appeared, and at Matt's question, Rita turned a cold smile upon Fleur. "Yes, do tell us. I can catch the fragrance even over here."

Fleur's puzzled frown gave way suddenly to a smile of relief. That everyone should be making such a fuss over something as insignificant as a perfume, while she was worried about a thousand-year-old bowl, struck her as ludicrous. "It's the bath oil I used last night. It has quite a staying power." She turned an amused glance toward Matt. "Do you like it?"

"No."

The abruptness of his answer unsettled

160

Fleur. "I thought it was rather too heavy myself," she began, but her words died when Matt without acknowledging her remark turned to Spandell.

"Do you want the camera from the truck?"

"I will eventually," replied Eric, "but first I'll use this one for the shots of the serpents. Will you handle the light meter?"

Fleur stood blinking in the sunlight, feeling a bit like a naughty child whom everyone had suddenly decided to ignore. "I think I'll have a look at the ball court," she said after a moment.

Rita said at once: "I'll come with you."

The thought of trying to concentrate on the ancient playing field with Rita in tow and Matt turned off by heaven knew what unsettled Fleur even more, but she turned a bright smile on the other woman. "Good. Maybe you won't mind filling me in on what went on there when the field was actually in use."

"Gladly," said Rita affably, but the moment they were out of sight of the men, the gloss vanished, and Fleur, noticing the leaden dislike that deepened the green of Rita's eyes, was reminded suddenly of the red jaguar that had earlier aroused that

161

peculiar feeling of uneasiness inside the temple.

"The game they played was a little like soccer, wasn't it?" she said, hoping the tremor in her voice was not too apparent.

"The two are comparable, yes." Rita pointed out a pair of parallel walls running the length of the field. "The spectators sat there."

As they drew nearer the walls, Fleur saw they were intricately carved in a kind of mural. Figures of players wearing feathered headdresses advanced from either end. In the middle they met, and there a skull with stone vapor rising from its jaws presided austerely.

"The death sign," Rita said with a note of satisfaction.

Fleur shivered though the sun was baking her back

"The victorious team cut off the head of a member of the other team." Rita laid a sharply pointed fingernail on a carved stream rising with six others from a decapitated neck. "The rest of the team was sacrificed to Kukulcan."

"The feathered serpent," Fleur managed.

Rita lifted an inquiring eyebrow. "You look a little pale. Does gore upset you?"

Fleur took a breath. "Not in stone. But

162

one would scarcely care to incorporate it in a dress design, so it doesn't especially interest me."

Rita's answer came back instantly. "Your interests are certainly not confined solely to dress designs."

"You're right," said Fleur smoothly. Rita meant Matt, of course, but Fleur was not about to admit to that understanding. "I find jewelry equally fascinating."

Rita turned away abruptly, and for a few minutes they toured the field in silence. When they came upon an odd-looking wall at the east end of the ball court, she said curtly, "That's the Platform of the Skulls. See? They're embedded in the cement."

Fleur stared. "Actual skulls?"

Rita turned up her mouth in cold amusement. "Probably those of the sacrificial victims." She ran her hand almost lovingly across the brow of one. "Teammates."

Feeling a ripple of gooseflesh up her arms, Fleur made as if to turn away, but Rita stepped suddenly into her path, ominously blocking her passage. "Matt is a descendent of these people, you know."

"Really?" So at last they were getting to the real reason Rita had tagged along. "His father was Irish, I believe."

"And his mother *mestizo*. Surely you've guessed that."

Fleur had, but she let the comment pass.

"He's quite hot-blooded," Rita said with sudden sharpness, her green eyes glittering. "I wouldn't cross him if I were you."

"I have no intention of doing so. Nor any reason to." There was the bowl. But there was no need for Rita to know of that.

"We had a grand time last night." Rita's expression had turned smug. To Fleur, the moment was irresistible.

"At a funeral?"

Rita's mouth tightened. "It was a rosary, not a funeral, as you very well know. Furthermore, the fun came later."

Fleur smiled sweetly. "Matt can be a charming host." Lifting a finger, she pointed idly toward an odd-looking structure where sculpted birds and beasts crouched greedily together. "What is that?"

Rita gave the carved piece a cursory glance. "The Platform of the Eagles and The Tigers." Her gaze returned to fasten malignantly on the cameo softness of Fleur's oval face. "They're eating human hearts."

Chapter Thirteen

Several days passed uneventfully. Though Fleur had meant each morning to find an opportunity to speak privately with Matt, she found herself inventing reasons not to. Try as she might, she could never manage to picture herself actually confessing to Matt that the Vera Cruz bowl had vanished. The longer she considered the possibility of a robbery having been committed, the less plausible the idea became, and without that straw to grasp, she felt entirely defenseless.

Another reason she found herself shying away from an encounter with Matt was the continuing enlargement within her mind of the picture Rita had painted of the evening she and Matt had spent together after the rosary for Ramon's brother.

Before Fleur had managed to escape from her at the Platform of the Eagles and Tigers, Rita had detailed a moonlight ride to the neighboring village of Cristo Cruces, tall glasses of tequila spiked with lime juice, a mariachi band that had played for them alone to dance, and a ride home, which, according to Rita, had included a number of stops, the nature of which she did not disclose, but referred to instead with a smirk of satisfaction.

After Rita's bizarre behavior at Chichén and Matt's peculiar treatment of Fleur when he had caught the scent of the bath oil, she felt like a combination pariah and recluse and devised a tactic to insure that she followed a path separate from the others each day.

Every morning after breakfast she busied herself in the library until Rita, Eric, and Matt had announced definite plans, and then she hurried off in the opposite direction. One morning she spent in a return visit to the ruins at Dzibilchaltun where she wandered contentedly into all the nooks and crannies that had escaped her the first time.

Though she would not, of course, reproduce the deformities of the Seven Clay Dolls, she did design a charming necklace using the primitive structure of the dolls in their wholeness. She envisioned the figures painted in the startling vividness of Mexican art and matched with sweaters and scarves striped in identical shades.

True to his word, Matt had procured samples of zapote wood, which were delivered to her the second morning after their trip to Progreso, and from these she had spent two afternoons doing some experimental carving.

Another half day she spent beside the Well of Sacrifice at Chichén, gazing thoughtfully into the dull muddiness while an iridescent clock-bird fanned its pendulum tail and strutted precariously atop the chalk-white walls of the cenote.

How many helpless victims had been thrust to their deaths from this spot? she wondered. According to the wide-eyed Antonia, a witch called Hechicera still lived in a cave at the bottom of the well. Because Hechicera had once loved a man she could not marry, she took out her frustrations on unwary creatures by drawing them to the murky depths with her magic powers and then turning them into the *alux* people Matt had mentioned on the way to Mérida.

How long ago that day seemed! In a way, Fleur reflected, she was glad there was only one more week left of her stay in the Yucatán. The dreams she had allowed herself to spin on the way back to the hacienda from Progreso had come to nothing.

Even if the bowl had not disappeared, she had made a tactical error she saw now. Instead of sitting placidly in the living room and allowing Matt and Rita to drive away to Lapaleta, she should have invited herself along as brazenly as Rita had done. Matt had shown signs of finding himself that day, and she, Fleur, had abandoned him. As Eric put it, Rita had her claws in him now, and Fleur, paralyzed by the guilt she felt over the missing bowl, seemed powerless to draw him back to her.

She went on brooding at the well until late afternoon and then made her way reluctantly back toward the hacienda. Pulling into the driveway, she was surprised to see Matt sunk in a lawn chair at the edge of the terrace. When he saw her, he rose quickly as if he had been waiting for her.

"Enough of avoiding me, young lady," he said when she had stepped down from the jeep. The mouth she longed for was smiling, and the dark eyes were lit with gaiety. "You and I are going to have a swim and a good talk." The lips moved perilously close to her own, the voice fell to a whisper. "I've missed you."

Fleur's heart pumped wildly. Did she dare believe that? "I'd love a swim."

"Good! Go and change then." He halted on the stone steps, his dark eyes glowing down at her. "Wait. I have a better idea," he murmured. "Let's go back to Progreso."

She laughed. "Now? But it's almost dinnertime."

He shrugged. "So what? I'll cook again." His voice turned playful. "Wouldn't you like that?"

"Yes, if you do as well as last time." His smile was irresistible. "But we'd be so late getting back, and I've a long day mapped out tomorrow." Swimming together here at the hacienda was one thing; spending hours alone at Progreso was quite another.

Matt hesitated, obviously disappointed. Then smiling again, he agreed. "Another time then. But at least let's make the most of a swim here."

When Fleur returned, attractively clad in a pale green bikini that set off her dark hair and fair skin, he was sitting at the poolside, his own muscular frame shimmering in the late afternoon sun.

"Sorry, but I couldn't wait to hit the water." His eyes moved appreciatively over her trim figure. "But now I'd be content simply to sit and stare."

Pleased, but slightly embarrassed by his frank appraisal, Fleur slid quickly into the pool. "Oh, lovely!" she said, bobbing up again.

He had entered the water too, and now beneath it she felt his strong hands encircling

169

her waist. "I want to know why you've been avoiding me."

"I seem to remember your avoiding *me,*" she said teasingly, but wished she had not when she saw how quickly his dark eyes clouded.

"You mean that day at Chichén when you were wearing that scent? I'm sorry I was rude."

"You weren't. Just abrupt."

His hands tightened, and she felt herself being drawn toward him through the cool water. "That was Mrs. Flaxendon's scent," he said. "I hope it isn't one of your favorites."

So that was it. She had reminded him of his stepmother. "Not at all. It was only a bath oil I came across in the towel closet. I suppose she left it there."

"I doubt it. Yours is one of the guest rooms. Hers was the one Rita is occupying."

"I see. Well, perhaps Mrs. Flaxendon lent it to a guest. Anyway, it doesn't matter. The fragrance was too heavy for me. I shan't be wearing it again."

His smile was apologetic. "I shouldn't have mentioned it, but it does bring back unpleasant memories. As I told Rita, that particular essence and the color violet, which my father's wife constantly wore, will forever be anathema to me, I'm afraid."

Rita knew he hated the perfume? How long had she known?

"Fleur?"

She started, realizing she had missed his question. "I'm sorry. I was wool-gathering. What did you say?"

"I said I thought you might have been upset with me because Rita and I were so late getting back the night of Ramon's brother's rosary."

"Was it late? I didn't notice." Not the whole truth, Fleur thought ruefully, but true enough that she had been too busy searching for the bowl to consult her watch.

"We took home a carload of relatives who just happen to live in every direction on the plains."

"I see. I thought you might have amused yourselves dancing or in some other way. After such a sad occasion, you might have needed to lift your spirits."

He laughed. "Rita did suggest dancing, but we settled on a drink when we'd deposited the last of the relatives." His eyes rested warmly on hers. "If you remember, I'd had no sleep the night before, and I was dying to get home and to bed."

Who was telling the truth? Matt or Rita?

171

The water seemed suddenly chilly, and Fleur pulled herself up on the tile coping, wrapping herself in a towel. Matt had lied about the hangover; perhaps he was lying now too. But Rita had behaved so ghoulishly at Chichén, who could believe her? Had she put the oil in the towel closet? Was she capable of such childishness?

"Fleur." Matt's finger gently turned her chin toward him, startling her back to the moment. "The incident with the perfume isn't the real reason you've been avoiding me, is it?"

Fleur corralled her thoughts. "I've been busy."

"Couldn't I have been invited to go along?"

"You have your own work to do."

His quiet gaze moved over her face and settled disconcertingly upon her eyes. "I'm between projects. You know that."

When Fleur did not reply, he went on. "Have you come to think differently of me since the day we spent at Progreso?"

"Of course not. It's..."

He waited.

"It's Rita," she said finally. "I think it's best not to taunt her."

His brows drew together in a puzzled frown. "I don't understand."

"She has to feel in command. You know
– the center of things." How much so, Fleur
was just beginning to find out!

"And when you and I go off together," he
said slowly, "she gets angry. Is that it?"

"Yes."

"Then what you're saying is you'd rather
please Rita than me."

Fleur was beginning to feel trapped. "I'm
not saying that at all. I just want the project
to go smoothly. When she's upset, it
doesn't."

"Umm. Well, I can understand that
much." He sighed. "She's been nagging me
for days to let her examine the Vera Cruz
bowl."

Fleur's heart stopped.

"The one you're studying," he went on.
"I told her she could have it as soon as you've
finished, but nothing seems to satisfy her."

Fleur opened her mouth to speak, but no
words came.

"But let's not talk about Rita." He put his
arm around her. "I want to know if you'll let
me tag along wherever it is you're going
tomorrow."

Fleur found her voice at last, though the
sound it produced was less than confident.
"I've told you. I don't want to upset Rita."

"She'll never know. Tell me where you're
173

going, and I'll come along after she and Eric have left." He smiled. "How is that?"

If they did spend the day together, perhaps she could find the right moment to explain about the bowl. "Very well. The Temple of the Dwarf at Uxmal."

"I'll be there before ten."

A rasping sound came from the direction of the lane, and the pickup wheezed into the driveway, its lights picking out the two of them sitting close together in the twilight's first gloom. The door slammed.

"Hello," Matt called out, but there was no answer, and in a moment Rita's figure appeared in the porch light and then vanished behind a second slammed door.

Matt gave a low whistle. "Well, come along." He put out his hand. "Let's go have dinner with the dragon."

The three of them dined alone. Eric was engaged in his darkroom and sent word not to wait for him. Surprisingly, Rita seemed to have dismissed the bad temper she had displayed earlier and chattered on agreeably about her day, her face animated, and her green eyes lit with disturbing sparks of a deeper hue that unaccountably sent little shivers of apprehension down Fleur's spine.

Toward the end of the meal, after a rather lengthy discourse on Rita's part concerning

174

the Conch Tower at Chichén and its possible use as an observatory, Fleur remembered suddenly what Eric had said about Rita's spurts of gaiety. She was most deadly then, he had warned.

Fleur looked up quickly and found Rita's glacial stare boring into her. "I've been most interested in examining the Vera Cruz bowl." Rita's tone was friendly, but there was steel beneath it.

Fleur returned her attention to the salad. "So Matt mentioned."

"Matt may lend it to us for the exhibition."

"Oh?" Fleur swallowed with difficulty. "Wonderful. It's quite handsome."

"When will you be finished with it?"

The words, more in the form of a shot than a question, laid bare the pleasant tenor of the meal.

Fleur paled. "I'm not certain."

Leaning back in her chair, Rita tapped a pointed finger on the stem of her water glass. "I can't imagine what's taking you so long. You can only be interested in the color."

Fleur forced composure into her voice. "The color is highly complex."

"There's no rush," Matt broke in. "You've still a week to consider the bowl, Rita, and as I said before, you may take it

175

when you return to Philadelphia if you choose."

"You'd really trust me with such a valuable piece?" Rita turned her cool green gaze on Matt. "The bowl can't be replaced, you know."

Fleur felt the room closing in on her and was grateful when Matt pushed back his chair signaling the end of the meal. "I'm well aware of its value, Rita." There was a note of irritation in his voice. "I also know you're an archaeologist of indisputable reputation. The bowl is as safe with you as it would be in a vault of the British Museum."

But it wasn't safe with me! Fleur felt the blood rushing from her head and steadied herself on the edge of the table.

"Are you all right?" Matt sent out a quick hand to catch her shoulder.

Fleur smiled weakly. "Quite. I got a bit too much sun today perhaps. I think I'll call it a day."

"Oh, I *am* sorry!" Rita appeared truly concerned. "It seems rather late in the year for sunstroke." She looked at Fleur. "But perhaps if one isn't used to it..." Her voice trailed away.

"I'll see you to your door," said Matt, but Rita halted them with a new anxiety in her voice. "I know you don't feel well, Fleur, but

176

if the two of you could wait in the living room for just a few minutes, there's something I simply must have your opinion on before tomorrow."

"Can't it wait?" said Matt.

"No, no." Fleur turned back toward the living room. "It's all right. I'm quite able to stay up as long as you like, Rita."

"Good!" Rita flashed a bright smile. "I won't be a moment."

Fleur and Matt moved together into the living room and settled on a couch before a glass-topped table.

"Are you sure you're not still feeling faint?" Matt's worried frown twisted Fleur's heart.

"I'm quite all right, really." What would he say if he knew what the real trouble was? Maybe she should have confessed everything at the dinner table, but the idea of being stampeded into an explanation by Rita had been too distasteful. Fleur wanted to be alone with Matt when she tried to explain what had happened.

Within a few minutes Rita appeared again. Matt had gone to the sideboard for a glass of sherry and stood with his back to her, but at the sound of Rita's voice, he turned.

She stood very straight and slim, her hands cupped together before her as if she

177

held a gift. "I'm afraid I have bad news," she said quietly. "I think it might be well if you sat down, Matt."

Chapter Fourteen

Afterward Fleur remembered thinking as she gazed at Rita poised in the doorway. *Such melodrama!* She remembered the peculiar posture of Rita's hands, and she remembered her own faint amusement at the parallel her mind drew between the sinewy form of the young archaeologist and Antonia's lurking Hechicera clutching victims in the depths of the cenote. But what happened for a few moments after Rita crossed the room and parted her palms on the glass top of the table, Fleur could not remember at all.

She was able to recall only the sight of half a dozen jagged pieces of the Vera Cruz bowl spilling across the table's shining surface, her own involuntary gasp, and Matt's shocked growl of disbelief.

If Matt spoke further, or if Rita said anything, Fleur had no recollection. In all her attempts later to put the evening back together, her mental processes moved painfully around several moments of nothing until they stumbled at last on the sound of her own voice, echoing tonelessly in the tomblike silence of the room. "Where did you find those?"

"In Antonia's trash hamper," Rita replied coldly.

As if he were still caught in the dream of the smashed bowl that had haunted him weeks before, Matt crossed the room in slow motion. In a moment that lasted forever, he put out his hand and picked up one of the fragments. "This is what we waited here for?" His eyes lifted to Rita's face. "This is what required an opinion?"

"God, no!" said Rita hastily. "I went to get reference notes. When I couldn't find them, I searched the hamper and found the broken bowl instead." She turned to look at Fleur, her eyes gleaming triumphantly. "I trust you have some kind of explanation."

Before Fleur could answer, Matt said in a hollow voice, "None is needed." Then without a glance at either of them, he strode from the room.

Fleur leaped up. "Matt! Wait! You must listen to me!"

Rita caught her arm. "I'd leave him alone if I were you."

"Well, you're not me!" Fleur tore herself

free. "You may have convinced Matt I broke the bowl and hid the pieces." Her cameo skin shone scarlet. "But I know differently. And so do you!"

Fleur found Matt hunched on a bench in a cluster of coco palms and rubber trees beyond the pool. A small fountain sang there, and Matt sat beside it staring at the dancing water marked with light from a nearly full moon.

"Matt." She sank beside him. "You must listen to me."

He turned dazed eyes upon her. "You expect me to listen now? Why didn't you tell me this afternoon you had broken the bowl?"

"Because I *didn't* break it!"

"It smashed of its own accord, I suppose."

"I don't know what happened! I only know when I went to look for it the night you and Rita went to Lapaleta, I couldn't find it. I haven't seen it since." She swallowed. "Not until just now in the living room."

"You've known since Sunday it was missing?" His stare was incredulous. "All the time, and you've said nothing?"

Tears had begun to mark her face. "I was

sure it was in my room somewhere. I kept looking, hoping."

"Hoping you wouldn't have to tell me you just happened to have misplaced a two-thousand-year-old Vera Cruz glaze?"

Her voice fell to a whisper. "I couldn't bear to tell you. Not while there was the slightest chance it might be recovered."

His jaw tightened. "Do you know the worth of that bowl?"

"I know it's invaluable. Oh, Matt! I haven't words to tell you how wretched I feel! But you must believe me. I did not break it."

"You were responsible for its safe-keeping."

She raised an anguished face to his. "Don't you think I know that? But what can I do? What can I say? What's happened is inexcusable, but it happened without my knowledge. Someone removed the bowl from my room."

His scornful laugh echoed against the paving stones. "Who would do that? Antonia? A clay dish from a street bazaar would please her better. Josie? Ramon? They're loyal servants. They would never betray my trust."

Fleur felt her throat close on hot tears. "And you think I would?"

"You have!"

"You won't at least give me the benefit of the doubt?"

"I gave you my bowl." His face was stone. "Isn't that enough?"

Fleur reeled from his words. "I realize that in your eyes I've done an unpardonable thing. I realize the bowl can never be duplicated, but –" her voice broke "– for you to turn against me without even considering my side . . ."

"My dear young lady." Matt got to his feet, eyes ablaze. "In the whole world there are only twenty-three Vera Cruz pieces extant." He stared at her for an endless moment. "Correction. Twenty-two!"

Fleur could hear his footsteps crossing the tile terrace by the pool, the sound of a motor starting. In a few seconds, the headlights of the jeep swept the treetops and then there was silence.

Fleur sank back on the bench. After a time she felt a touch on her sleeve, and turning, found Eric Spandell seated beside her.

He spoke softly. "I was coming out of the darkroom. I heard."

Fleur released a ragged breath. "Rita is responsible."

"Of course. I tried to warn you."

182

"But Eric! The Verz Cruz bowl! How *could* she?"

"She'd do anything to get her way. I told you that."

"I can't believe it."

"Yet you have to." Eric's sardonic smile twisted his face. "What now?"

"If you heard, you know," she answered dully. "Nothing. Matt will never forgive me."

Eric was silent.

"Unless –" Fleur lifted her head. "Unless I can convince him Rita has done this sort of thing before."

"In other words, you want me to help you."

"Will you?"

"No." The answer was flat, unequivocal.

"Eric! How can you not!"

He stood up. "I'm here to do a job. I'm doing it – and well, too – but if I allow myself to get tangled up in Rita's vengeance, she'll bring me down. I'm sorry, but you'll have to find a way out by yourself."

Fleur stared. "But Eric! I'm not asking just for me. Rita mustn't be allowed to go on destroying things – destroying people's lives! – and get away with it. You should have seen her triumph in there. She's mad!"

183

Eric shrugged. "Sorry," he muttered again and turned away.

After what seemed hours, the jeep returned, and Fleur still seated in the shadows, had difficulty suppressing the desire to call out and try once more to win Matt's forgiveness. But there was no hope of that, she knew, and she watched numbly until the lights in the living room went out.

The longer she thought about it, the more incredible the situation became. That a supposedly civilized woman would stoop to such vile trickery because of jealousy was simply not to be believed! Yet it was true.

An archaeologist had deliberately smashed a two-thousand-year-old bowl that could never be replaced. It seemed impossible that Rita's desire for Matt could override her professional sensitivities to such an extent, but Fleur had seen the shattered fragments. Matt had held one in his hand.

Fleur felt physically ill. The malignity of the woman! The hatred that had spawned that act. More than anything Fleur longed to pack her bags, to be gone far from this place where she was so despised, not only by Rita, but now by Matt as well. The one person she might have counted on for help was Eric, and he had turned his back on her too.

But even if she could manage somehow to stick it out there for the one remaining week, ignoring Rita's slurs and Matt's icy anger, how could she live with her own humiliation? She had betrayed a trust, and the betrayal was irrevocable.

The best thing to do was to leave in the morning. Surely Spandell would at least have courage enough to drive her into Mérida.

But what of Flaxendon? What would happen to his plans for the exhibition if she quit now? He had trusted her too, a complete unknown. Aside from the money he had already spent, he was counting on her to make a commercial success of the Mayan showing. She could finish the designs, of course. She had more than enough material to do that, but seeing the show through would entail several more months of work with Rita in Philadelphia. If she walked out now, any possibility of future dealings between the two of them would be impossible.

But weren't they already impossible? She could never hold her tongue with Rita now. To do so would be the same as admitting defeat, of acknowledging that Rita had outsmarted her, and she had taken it lying down.

Fleur's cheeks burned in the moonlight.

Was there no way to resolve this dilemma?

A night bird called from the undergrowth beyond the pool. The lonesome sound was the same one she had heard a number of times since her arrival. She had grown accustomed to it, and often thought she heard in its muted tones a tranquility that was truly beautiful, but tonight the beauty was overlaid only with despair.

Putting her hands to her ears, Fleur stumbled through the shadows to the house. In her room she undressed quickly by the light shining from the bathroom, wishing her troubles could slip from her as easily as her clothing.

From the drawer where the bowl should have rested in safety, she drew the first nightgown her hand touched: a filmy trifle Barbara had given her as a going away present. Slipping it over her shoulders, she sank on the end of the bed, too weary to stay up any longer and too wretched to hope for sleep.

Restlessly, she rose and went to stand at the glass door, looking out on the patio. Across it, a light glowed in Matt's window. He was still up. What was he thinking?

Gradually a sense of the injustice of her predicament came over her. None of this was really her fault. Matt had offered the bowl to her, pressed it upon her, in fact, in spite of her objections. She had wrapped it carefully and put it in a safe place. That Rita had found that place and removed the bowl was Rita's crime, not hers.

It was true, of course, that she could have examined the elusive shades of orange immediately and returned the glazed piece to Matt the next morning. If only she had! But there was no hurry, Matt had said, and they had been very busy.

The hectic pace of the last several weeks should not be overlooked either as playing a part in this dismal situation. Touring the ruins all day, studying half the night. She had worked very hard, and she knew her designs were good.

Why should she throw all that away just because of one vicious woman? The success of this job was certain to open new doors of opportunity. Aside from the growth of her career, Fleur thought of her need for the money. If she withdrew now, Flaxendon would, of course, cancel her contract, and even if he made use of some of her designs, the fact that she had reneged on their agreement would always cast a shadow over her reputation.

And finally there was Matt.

She glanced across at the window, now

darkened. Could she really bring herself to leave him without a reconciliation? Except for Rita's arrogant willfulness, they might be in each other's arms this moment, nurturing the emotions aroused that day at Progreso.

With a sigh, she turned from the glass door, and reluctantly pulling back the cool sheet, climbed into bed. A great weariness settled over her. Perhaps in the morning when she woke, the world would look different. Perhaps in the morning she would know what to do.

Chapter Fifteen

When Fleur woke in the morning, her thoughts flew at once to her hope of the night before that somehow, surrounded by sunlight and refreshed by sleep, she would have an answer to her problem.

Did she?

A whole flock of butterflies flitted about inside her stomach while she drew a bath and contemplated facing Matt and Rita. Her eye fell on the vial of bath oil Matt so despised. It seemed a bad omen to be reminded at this particular moment of Rita's perfidy.

Submerging herself to the chin in the warm water, Fleur tried to reconstruct Rita's uninvited entry into her room. Undoubtedly it must have occurred the day she and Matt had spent in Progreso.

She had gone over and over in her mind the days preceding that one, and she could not recall a single time she had opened the lingerie drawer and not felt the reassuring roundness of the bowl tucked out of sight among her underthings. Not until the night when she had reached for it and found it missing.

That was the night, too, when she had first discovered the bath oil. Evidently Rita had brought it with her, rummaged through Fleur's things, and finding the bowl, left the vial in exchange for the Vera Cruz glaze.

Had she intended breaking the bowl from the start? Or had Matt's increased attentions toward Fleur given her the idea?

Fleur stared unseeing at her toes wavering beneath the water. What did any of it matter now? The bowl was broken, and like Humpty Dumpty, could never be put together again. But at least her relationship with Matt held some possibility of mending if she could only find some way to make him listen to her.

He had asked to meet her today at the Temple of the Dwarf. That was before he knew about the bowl, of course, but his moods changed with lightning swiftness. He, too, had had all night to reconsider. Perhaps he would appear at Uxmal after all, and if so, the chance was good he would listen to reason.

Stepping from the tub, Fleur quickly dried her narrow hips with a soft towel. The bath had subdued the restless butterflies, but one nagging thought more akin to a persistent gnat still tormented her. Even if she and Matt were able to settle their differences, how would they handle Rita's fury?

For a moment she stared thoughtfully at the murky contents of the vial of bath oil. Then she plucked it swiftly from the shelf and tossed it into the wastebasket. Instead of dawdling, she should be dressing. The sooner she got down to breakfast, the quicker the whole problem would be resolved.

Armed with fresh resolution, Fleur slipped into her jeans and a light-blue top with a cowl collar. She was relieved her reflection in the mirror showed no signs of strain, and she tried her brightest smile. Confidence was half the game, she reminded herself.

190

This was a new day. Anything was possible.

Matt, Rita, and Spandell were already into breakfast when Fleur appeared, and though she heard laughter and a spirited exchange of voices as she came down the hall, when she entered the dining room, a strained silence fell over the table and remained unbroken until Fleur herself spoke.

"Will anyone be using the jeep today?"

"I'd planned to," Spandell said, helping himself to a serving of eggs without meeting Fleur's glance. "I'm going back to Chichén for more shots of the Chacmools."

"Matt and I are taking the pickup," Rita announced with aloof assurance, passing her cup to Eric for more coffee.

Fleur glanced quickly at Matt. He was going with Rita? He met her gaze for a moment, and then looked away.

"I can take the ranch wagon then," said Fleur evenly. "Or the car."

Without looking at her Matt replied, "I've sent one of the hands off in the wagon to get supplies, and I'm afraid the battery is dead in the car."

Fleur fixed her gaze on her plate and began to eat mechanically. Rita had not said where she and Matt were going, but it didn't matter. Plainly, Fleur was not invited. Nor

191

had Eric offered to take her with him. They were squeezing her out.

Lifting her cup, she swallowed painfully, aware that tears hovered dangerously close to her lashes. But Matt must not see how deeply he had hurt her. Pretending she was alone at the table, she shut out their voices and set her mind to the task of planning what to do. One thing was certain. They would not drive her away!

Tomorrow she would put in her bid for a vehicle earlier and make the trip to Uxmal. There were still portions of the Chichén ruins, particularly the view of the feathered serpents, she wanted to sketch. And she could go to Dzibilchaltun one more time. The days would pass.

But if she weren't allowed transportation, she could handle that too. If worse came to worst, she could do the serpent sketches from her reference books and wind up the whole week without going anywhere.

The pretense carried her through the tedious meal, and she even managed a brief smile as she excused herself. Before she had gotten as far as the living room door, however, Eric caught up with her.

"I'll be moving around a lot today," he said half-apologetically. "I'll need to work alone."

"Certainly," she said, pleased that her voice did not betray either her contempt for him or her feelings of depression. "I need to do the same." With another brief smile, she passed him and went down the corridor to her room.

The morning passed slowly. Fleur took her work out into the patio as soon as she was certain the others had gone, but the unsettled feelings that had followed her from the breakfast table multiplied in the silence of the hacienda, and she found herself wishing desperately she could find some manner of escape with honor.

Just before noon an idea occurred to her, and when Josie brought out her luncheon tray, Fleur detained her for a moment. "There's a train that passes through Lapaleta, isn't there, Josie?"

"*Sí, señorita.*" The placid cook smiled. "Morning and evening."

"Would it take me to San Cristobal?"

Josie frowned. "*Sí.* But that is several days' journey, I think."

Fleur could see the peasant woman had never been to San Cristobal herself and was uncertain about the distance. "I have some time free for travel, and I'd like to leave this afternoon, but I have no way to get to

193

Lapaleta. Do you think Ramon could drive me?"

Josie's face broke into a wide grin. "In the white car? *Ay, sí, señorita!* He would be most honored."

And most delighted at the opportunity of backing the Cadillac out of the garage for a real journey instead of a mere polishing, thought Fleur with a smile. "Tell him I'd like to leave in an hour then."

When Fleur finished lunch, she went quickly back to her room and tossed several changes of clothing into a light bag. The trip to San Cristobal was the perfect solution. She would not have to confront Matt or Rita, she could postpone her decision about whether or not to go on to Philadelphia, and still she would not be admitting defeat at Rita's hands.

With her sketchbook under her arm, she returned to the entry hall, where she hastily scrawled a note addressed to no one in particular, but simply stating she had taken the train to San Cristobal and would return later in the week.

Chapter Sixteen

All the way to San Cristobal, Fleur fought a desire to go back over in her mind the events that had occurred since her arrival in the Yucatán, and in particular, those of the last few days.

It would be so easy – the natural thing, in fact – to spend these days of escape rehashing the experiences of yesterday. But what was more important now, she kept reminding herself, was tomorrow. Where was she going when she left the Yucatán. Up in her career, or on the skids professionally and emotionally because of Rita Pittman?

These few days away from the hacienda would best be spent in regrouping, in deciding which was more important, giving in to her desire to have Matt at any cost, a decision that would mean digging in her heels and fighting Rita Pittman, or facing the fact that Matt had not trusted her enough or cared enough for her to stand by her or at least to listen to her explanations.

Jostling along the bumpy rails, Fleur found simply putting the truth into words painful, but the actual assimilation of the full impact of it was unbearable. Unseeing, she stared through the train window at the passing landscape, wondering if she would ever again feel as lighthearted and joyous as she had the day she and Eric Spandell had ridden down from Mérida together.

She had not known Matt then, except by reputation. She had not known the consuming blaze of those dark eyes, the tantalizing curve of his mouth, or his arms pressing her to the taut leanness of his body.

She had not known the fierceness of his temper either, she reminded herself stubbornly. Or his almost ruthless impatience. Perhaps, after all, Rita had done her a favor turning Matt against her. Perhaps she was well out of it.

Sighing, she forced her attention toward the other passengers, her designer's eyes noting automatically the physical splendor of the *mestizo* men, the slanting jawlines, the high cheekbones, the aquiline noses. Matt had such a nose.

Matt.

Exasperated, she switched her gaze to the landscape, but wherever she looked, she saw his glowing eyes, the parted lips she could almost feel pressed against her own, the shock of dark hair . . .

When she had almost exhausted herself with unwelcome thoughts and the effort to rout them from her brain, the pink and sugar-white stones of San Cristobal's churches appeared at last beyond the window, and she sat forward eagerly, trembling with relief. Surely here in this strange city with no command of the language, she would be obliged to focus all her energies on communication and the simple tasks of existence. There would be no time for regrets or remonstrances or for dwelling on her separation from the one man she had ever met who made life whole for her.

To some extent, her wish that San Cristobal, like a magic carpet, might whisk her up and away from the trials and pressures of life at the hacienda came true. As soon as she stepped from the train, she was at once caught up in the picturesque life of the city. She wandered captivated through the narrow streets, eyeing with admiration the proud Indians on horseback come to sell their produce in the busy markets, their ponchos gracefully draping short pants and exposing their brown legs to the crisp air.

She trod the sidewalks, her rubber-soled shoes mingling with thick-soled leather sandals fastened loosely on the sturdy feet of peasants. She breathed the smells of the market, and as eagerly as any tourist examined its wares, watching in fascination while a young boy shaped clay with deft brown fingers and an old woman ladled wax over wicks suspended from a wheel turning slowly above a cauldron, moment by moment adding to vivid stacks of candles spread about her feet.

For a day and a half she roamed at will, stopping to sketch the piquant face of a child or the sprawled form of a boy napping under a donkey cart. She drew the women, trailing at a respectful distance behind their men, their black heads topped with beribboned straw hats, their white-toothed smiles flashing shyly in half-averted faces.

Memories of Matt's accusing face flashed before her now and again, but with less intensity than in the train, and by nightfall of the second day, seated in the dining room of the small hotel where she had taken a room, she felt calmer and more at ease with herself than she had in days.

It was during this meal she learned, through a chance conversation with the manager, of a cluster of ruins up in the mountains.

"Not many go there," the man said, setting a steaming dish of enchiladas before her. "No roads. The train is the only way. And very slow."

"I could get there and back in one day though?"

Sí, sí. You leave before daybreak. At dusk the train recrosses the mountain and returns to San Cristobal."

Before dawn, refreshed by a night of dreamless sleep, which she attributed to a tequila nightcap the jovial restaurateur had urged upon her, Fleur boarded the quaint little train whose destination for her was the ruins of Florenda.

Her fellow passengers were chiefly peasants from the mountains who had come down to San Cristobal for market day and were returning now to their remote homes laden with coconuts, live chickens tied together at the feet with strands of sisal, new straw sombreros, and bundles of coarse cloth peeping from ragged wrappings.

From the restaurateur's description, she had expected Florenda to be situated high in the mountains and had settled back for a long ride in the narrow little coach, when to her surprise the conductor passed through the car calling out "Florenda!" almost as soon as they had moved into the foothills.

Once on the platform with the train

already chugging out of sight, Fleur saw that the village overlooked a fertile valley, and beyond it a thick forest burst green and inviting. The ruins must be there, she decided, and after a halting conversation conducted chiefly with hands and vigorous noddings, she and a native, whose truck of ancient vintage sat idle at the door of the station, struck a bargain and set out.

The forest, though it appeared impenetrable, was crisscrossed by innumerable dirt trails and footpaths along which, to Fleur's delight, she glimpsed native women swathed in black, balancing the produce of their realm upon well-formed heads with shiny hair done up in knots. Around one bend she caught sight of a woman weaving, one end of the loom tied around her waist, and the other fastened to a tree trunk.

The further they penetrated the forest, the easier it was for Fleur to relegate the events at the hacienda to a dream state, and to breathe life anew in this fresh and invigorating atmosphere.

The ruins themselves were worth every creaking mile the laboring taxi traversed. Though the beauties of Chichén and Dzibilchaltun were still vivid in her mind, the carvings of these Mayan temples exceeded even those. Exquisite figures carved in stucco spoke eloquently of the civilization they represented. In one crypt she discovered the body of a priest-king elaborately clothed in crumbling garments, his face a jade-mosaic mask so beautiful Fleur stood in stunned silence revering the ancient artistry that had formed it. Other intricately carved stones cried out to be read, and regretfully she passed her hands over their uneven surfaces wishing that, like braille, they could speak to her fingertips.

For two more days she lingered in San Cristobal, coming daily with her Mexican guide to the quiet ruins where bit by bit her spirit and perspective returned. But on the morning of the third day she realized suddenly she had fallen into a routine so pleasant and undemanding she might, if she possessed the means, stay on forever, losing herself day by day in the ancient mysteries of her surroundings.

In truth, however, she did not have the means, nor the time, nor – finally – the inclination to remain. A challenge awaited her at the hacienda and she must face it. Thanks to the halcyon days here, she felt ready now to meet it.

When the train arrived in Lapaleta early on Friday morning, Fleur was surprised by the eagerness with which she welcomed the first sight of the ordinarily sleepy little town, and it was a few moments before she realized that an extraordinary hustle and bustle seemed to have taken possession of it in her absence.

Instead of placid storefronts where proprietors tipped back in chairs and napped contentedly between customers, every doorway was crowded with buyers and sellers; garlands of crepe paper festooned the balconies, and though it was scarcely nine o'clock, hordes of peasants maneuvered horses and wagons between an unusual number of motorized vehicles, many with license plates from other areas.

In all this confusion, Fleur wondered how long it would be before she was able to find someone with enough time on his hands to drive her out to the hacienda. She felt primed to meet Matt, and Rita too, and the thought of having to spend half the day or more hanging around in Lapaleta had a deflating effect on the enthusiasm of her return.

She was just about to approach an old man leaning against a donkey cart when she spied the white Cadillac parked in the shade of a rickety building across the narrow street from the train station and recognized the cocky figure of Ramon threading his way across the busy street.

A broad smile of delight broke across his face at seeing Fleur. Dodging a horsedrawn cart bearing two disgruntled pigs, he hurried toward her.

"Ah, Señorita Normandy! You have returned at last." Sweeping off his sombrero, he placed it reverently over his heart. "We have been much concerned for your safety."

Fleur blinked. "Why, what do you mean?"

Ramon's eyes rounded with the drama Fleur had learned to recognize as a characteristic of these exuberant Hispanic people. "There are *bandidos* in San Cristobal. Highwaymen!" He ran the fingernail of his thumb across his throat and rolled his brown eyes. "You have been gone many days."

Fleur laughed. "You're kind to have been concerned, but nothing with even a hint of peril happened to me. My biggest worry was whether I'd find a ride back to the hacienda."

"*Ay, sí, señorita!*" He swung his arm in the direction of the Cadillac. "Every day I have brought the car. And every day I must go home to Señor Kirkpatrick with the sad news that you do not return."

Fleur's heart leaped. "Señor Kirkpatrick was concerned?"

Ramon's brows met. *"Ay! Sí!* He has been very disturbed during your absence."

Fleur felt her mouth go dry. "By disturbed do you mean – angry?"

Ramon considered his answer. "Not so angry as when I have forgotten the gasoline and the car has stopped far out on the plain." He drew his brows together. "But more angry than when I have broken the fender of the white car on Dead Souls' Day."

"I see." Fleur sighed. "In that case, perhaps we should be getting back."

Ramon hoisted her bag onto his shoulder and led her through a snarl of traffic to the other side of the street.

"What's going on here?" Fleur asked.

"Fiesta!" said Ramon, grinning.

"I see. Then you'll be having a happy time tonight, I expect."

His smile faded. "I do not think so."

Fleur settled in the back seat. Perhaps she had been tactless. Ramon must still be mourning for his brother and not ready to participate in celebrations. She hoped she had not offended him.

In a few minutes, Ramon managed to raise an enormous cloud of dust, frighten two old crones in black shawls, and scatter a flock of chickens in his effort to turn the long car around in the middle of the block, but at last they were headed in the right direction and in less than half an hour the hacienda loomed ahead.

Matt was pacing in front of the swimming pool when Ramon turned into the driveway, and at the sight of him, Fleur felt a sudden, unexpected surge of joy.

Ramon was not so ecstatic. "He is waiting," he said in a guarded tone.

"So I see." Fleur's pleasure dimmed. Matt did look truly angry. "Was Miss Pittman around when you left earlier?"

"No, *señorita.*" Ramon halted the automobile a few feet from where Matt stood scowling. "She has gone with Señor Spandell to Uxmal."

Well, at least if she were in for a tongue-lashing, Rita would not be there to revel in it.

Ramon deposited her at the curb and speedily disappeared around the corner of the house. Matt stood with arms folded, watching her approach. "Welcome home," he said tonelessly when she drew even with him.

"Thank you." Dared she hope his first show of displeasure was for Ramon's benefit only? Fleur tried a tentative smile, but it was not returned. "Have you had breakfast?"

"Yes, on the train, thank you."

Nothing more was said until they had entered the hall, where Matt suddenly stepped in front of her, blocking her passage. "What made you do a damnfool thing like running off to San Cristobal?"

Fleur stiffened. "I wanted to see Florenda." That wasn't quite true, of course. She had never heard of the ruins of Florenda until the restaurateur made mention of them, but this was not the time to go into that.

"You shouldn't have gone unaccompanied."

"Why not? I encountered no danger."

"Danger!" He snorted. "Of course there was no danger."

"Ramon said –"

"If you aren't acquainted by this time with Ramon's melodramatic tendencies, you're rather a poor judge of character."

His superior tone brought a hot glow to Fleur's cheeks. "Why are you so concerned then?"

He turned an angry glare on her. "I think it was rather foolish for one unfamiliar with the true significance of the ruins to try to explore them unaided."

"In other words, you think I'm stupid to

206

have enjoyed them without somone to lead me around by the hand!" Fleur's gray eyes flashed. "Well, I'm sorry to disappoint you, but I found them fascinating. There are guidebooks, you know," she added in a withering tone. "Even the most humble among us can sometimes fathom the printed page."

A deep red suffused his cheeks, and his dark eyes burned like coals. "I assume you have your work well under control since you felt free to go skipping off on a holiday."

"It was a *working,* holiday, Dr. Kirkpatrick." The gray eyes snapped. "But as a matter of fact, I've completed my designs. I could leave tomorrow for Philadelphia."

She saw him pale. "You'd abandon your team?"

"On the contrary." Her voice throbbed with emotion. "It appears to me I have been abandoned by them."

"Because they've gone off to Uxmal?" he said patronizingly. "You weren't here to go with them."

Fleur brushed past him. There was no point to this argument. And if he was so angry with her, why was he wasting his time upbraiding her? Why not take himself off to the ruins and leave her to stew in her own

207

discomfort at having been dismissed by the master." I think I'll go and change, if you don't mind."

His blunt question stopped her. "What do you intend to do with the rest of the day?"

She turned, surprised. "Why do you ask?"

"I'm going to Progreso. I'd like you to come with me."

Fleur stared. First he bawled her out and then he extended invitations. "Why should I go there?"

"You seemed to enjoy it before."

"It was a pleasant enough day."

A shadow crossed his face, then vanished as swiftly as it had come. "We'd be back before the others return from Uxmal."

Was he so afraid of Rita he dared not cross her? Or so under her spell he did not want to?

"I have work to do here," Fleur reported.

An imitation smile twisted his lips. "You said your work was finished."

Caught in her own trap, Fleur flushed. "Then I'll be frank. I don't choose to go, thank you."

His jaw hardened. "As you will. But I'm afraid I cannot permit you the same freedom this evening."

"What do you mean?"

"I have accepted an invitation for the four of us to be honored guests at the fiesta in Lapaleta."

Fleur glared. "I'll accept my own invitations, if you don't mind."

A cold smile curved his lips. "You were not here to do so. As your host, I felt it was my privilege."

What would he have done, Fleur wondered if she had not come back this morning? But she let it pass. In all fairness he had – in all respects except those related to her personally – displayed a most gracious hospitality. If he required one evening of reciprocation on the part of his guests, the least she could do was to comply. "What time do we leave?"

"Shortly before five."

"I'll be ready."

Chapter Seventeen

The frenzy in the streets of Lapaleta when Matt, Rita, Eric, and Fleur arrived late in the afternoon presented an interesting blend of total abandonment to gaiety and a tightly restrained excitement quite similar, Fleur thought, to the held breath of a birthday child poised to puff at the candles on the long-awaited cake.

Everywhere there were the sounds of guitars and singing, trills of high-pitched laughter, and the pounding of hooves on the hard, dirt streets. Lusty vendors offered charred meat and pork cracklings to natives only too eager to turn the enticing smells to tastes. On every corner street-sellers hawked fuchsia-colored coconut and dripping ices tinted in outlandish colors.

A parade of quaint floats was lined up along one side of the main thoroughfare, and enormous papier-maché heads depicting wild-eyed bulls and mustachioed *bandidos* topped slender bodies of *mestizo* boys and girls. Busiest perhaps were the stalls selling hats, around which were crowded hordes of backwoods peasants intent on practical souvenirs.

Fleur held a thin woolen shawl around her shoulders, bared by a Mexican blouse of creamy lace and thin white lawn that attractively molded her firm young breasts. All the time she was dressing she had dreaded the upcoming encounter with Rita and the long evening she anticipated in her company, but much to her surprise, Rita had greeted her affably and was now chattering gaily with Matt while Fleur and Eric Spandell trailed behind them fending off exuberant children and their dripping confections.

"I'm glad I came," she confided in a low voice to Eric, who shuffled along muttering laconic observations and berating himself because he had left his camera behind. "But I'm wondering what our role of 'honored guests' will consist of." Eric shrugged. "Who knows. I just do as I'm told."

"So I've noticed," Fleur answered a bit sharply. If Eric had stood by her, it might be she instead of Rita on Matt's arm now. "Does compliance make you happy?"

Eric's small brown eyes bored into her. "About as happy as noncompliance makes you, I suppose."

"You mean my going off to San Cristobal?"

"The trip wasn't exactly in the itinerary, you know."

"There's nothing in my contract that says I can't strike out alone," Fleur replied with growing irritation.

"Perhaps not," Eric said in a lowered tone, "but you should have seen Matt's face when he read your note."

Fleur's heart skipped a beat. Matt could

pretend if he wanted that he objected only to the fact that she had toured the ruins without professional assistance, but she was almost sure he had missed her and that was the reason he was so angry and so insistent upon Ramon's meeting every train.

However, she thought with a fresh twinge of jealousy, certainly nothing in his present behavior indicated he was languishing for her. Up ahead, Matt had halted before a lavishly decorated float bearing a gold throne, which he was laughingly pointing out to Rita, his dark face close to her flushed cheek.

As Fleur and Spandell approached, Matt held out his hand to Rita as she mincingly mounted a set of make-do steps shoved up to the side of the float.

"Oh, no!" groaned Eric. "We're not going to ride on that thing, are we?"

Matt laughed. "Of course! We're going to lead the parade." His gaze rested for a moment on Fleur's bare shoulders and then moved to her lips. "Afterward, Don Esteban, the mayor, will honor us with a fiesta banquet in his home."

"How nice," murmured Fleur.

"Let me help you." She felt Matt's strong arm slip around her shoulder. An electric tremor seized her, and she felt the hand he

212

held tremble. "In response, his grip tightened, and for a moment they stood, glances locked, while Eric patted his foot impatiently on the packed earth of the street, and Rita glared from her throne.

Dazed at this sudden switch in behavior, Fleur heard him speak quietly. "I hope you'll find this evening enjoyable."

Though Matt's words were audible only to her, Fleur felt as if he had shouted an apology for the whole world to hear.

"I've already begun to do so," she said with a quiver in her voice. "Everything is so colorful, so exciting."

"Matt!" Rita's voice cut between them. "That fat little man in the red coat is signaling the start."

"Coming." Two strong hands closed about Fleur's waist and swung her over the edge of the float. "Behind Rita's chair is a supporting stand," he murmured. "We're to hold on to that, and you –" he turned a merry face on Spandell "– you're to man that pasteboard camera at the rear, I believe."

Groaning, Spandell clambered up, and in a moment the team of donkeys responsible for propelling the decorated encumbrance down the main street responded to a sharp cry from its master, and the parade got off to a lurching start.

A sea of grinning faces packed the sidewalks and spilled to the edge of the street. Fleur, who had never participated in a parade before, found herself caught up in its spirit. Who could resist such enthusiasm, such a wild waving of brown arms and cacophony of whistles?

The gala caravan of donkey-pulled floats and decorated bicycles traversed the length of the tiny town, turned around, circled the square three times, and finally came to a halt beside a ramshackle building Matt pointed out as the city hall.

"There'll be a presentation now. Gold keys or something," he added.

Rita laughed shrilly. If Fleur was enthusiastic, Rita was beside herself with the attentions of the crowd and responded with regal magnanimity each time a cheer was heard. Eric, who had maintained a stony countenance since the first lurch of the float, sighed heavily at Matt's announcement, but Fleur was of the opinion he was enjoying the festivities far more than he would admit.

As for Fleur, she felt as though she had suddenly sprouted wings and might rise and circle the town like some exuberant bird freed unexpectedly from its cage. Throughout the unsteady ride, Matt's arm had encircled her, the strong blunt fingers pressing her narrow waist intimately, while Rita, oblivious to what went on behind her, smiled and nodded with queenly attention to the applauding crowd.

All at once a slim, elderly man clothed in white from the tips of his boots to the broad sombrero shading his aristocratic features stepped through the front door of the city hall and began to speak in an eloquent manner, frequently punctuated with free-flowing gestures. The crowd responded with shouts of approval and bursts of raucous laughter.

"What's the hell's he saying?" muttered Eric, who appeared as tense as if he expected a hangman, or at the least a jailer, to issue from the building and place them all under arrest.

Almost without moving his lips Matt replied, "He's telling them how we've brought the dead back to life through our explorations of the ruins."

"Well, they don't seem too impressed," said Eric sourly.

"I think the whole thing is delightful," said Rita without disturbing the broad smile that she seemed to take such pleasure in bestowing upon the people.

The speech over at last, the elegantly attired little man, who turned out to be Don

Esteban himself, stepped forward and handed to Matt a silver box tied splendidly in multicolored ribbons.

The crowd shouted. "They want us to open it," said Matt. Leaning forward, he placed the box on Rita's lap. "Will you do the honors?"

Rita responded with delight, her smile broadening as her grasping fingers tugged at the ribbons.

The lid came off.

Straining forward to see, Fleur heard Rita's gasp and saw that the box would have tumbled from her lap had not Matt reached swiftly across her shoulder and rescued it.

Casting a piercing look at Rita's pale face, he lifted from the wrappings a squat little bowl that gleamed as brilliantly orange as the setting sun in his brown hand.

"A Vera Cruz glaze!" exclaimed Eric.

"Surely not!" Fleur stared.

"But it is!" Spandell insisted.

"No." Matt's eyes had not left Rita's face. "Only an excellent imitation." He lifted the bowl high for the eager spectators to see and bowed his thanks to Don Esteban. "A potter called Akumal makes them in limited quantities." His gaze bored into Rita. "For special customers."

Once more he lifted the bowl high, and

Fleur, casting a quick look at Rita, saw that the dead-white pallor that had come over her face when she opened the box was still there like a death mask on her normally florid skin.

"What's the meaning of this?" hissed Spandell in Fleur's ear.

"I have no idea," murmured Fleur, but a gradual flush of embarrassment was rising to cover her own cameo whiteness. Obviously Don Esteban had learned – probably from Matt – that Fleur had broken Matt's prized piece of the glaze, and this was an attempt to make amends for the carelessness of a gringo girl from New York.

Before anyone had noticed her discomfiture, however, they were caught up in a swirl of activity that brought them down from the float and into waiting vehicles by which they were transported out of town to the hacienda of Don Esteban.

In contrast to the shabbiness of the village, Don Estaban's home was a palace. Elaborate stucco porticos stretched across its front, the floor of which was tiled in brilliant Mexican glazes of every shade and hue. Inside, the walls were hung with fine paintings of old European masters, and the legs of heavily carved chairs stood deep in the pile of carpets with the texture of fur.

Fleur gazed about in wonder, and turning to Matt, she was about to comment on an exquisite carving of zapote wood when Rita pressed near and said in a strained voice, "The excitement has been rather much for me, I'm afraid. Please find Ramon and ask him to drive me home."

Matt surveyed her for an instant. Then, cupping her chin in his brown hand, he turned her face up to his. "You do look rather pale. Poor Rita."

Fleur felt herself grow cold. What manner of man *was* this? Did he enjoy manipulating women like puppets on a string, one minute devoting himself to Fleur while Rita dangled limply on the outskirts of his attentions, then switching his concentration to Rita, abandoning Fleur?

"I'm afraid I can't call Ramon," Fleur heard him say. He had released Rita's chin, but held her still with an arm about her shoulder. "I've excused Ramon until eleven o'clock for his own merrymaking." He glanced about at the revelers, some of whom were already displaying signs of overindulgence. "And I'd hardly trust a hired car on this night. But come." He squeezed her shoulder, his dark eyes full upon Rita's anxious face. "You'll feel better when you've eaten."

"I'm sure I won't!"

Fleur felt a moment of fleeting pity for the woman who had caused her so much misery. How awful to be ill in a stranger's house in the midst of so much gaiety. Fleur glanced at the man beside her. And how unfeeling of Matt not to make some arrangement to ease Rita's discomfort. Why, he was almost smiling!

She turned away abruptly. What a fickle beast he was! How was it possible that he had the power to change her into a simpering idiot with the touch of his hand or a hot glance? Well, tonight was the last time! Oh, if only tomorrow were the last day, and she could pack her bags and be forever free from Matt Kirkpatrick's duplicity.

For the remainder of the evening Fleur stewed inwardly, still managing to keep up a pleasant chatter with her dinner partner, a diplomat's eager young son having his first taste of Yucatecan customs. She took some comfort, too, in the knowledge that Ramon, who had gloomily predicted he would not be taking part in the festivities, was free for at least a few hours to enjoy himself.

Rita, she noticed however, was faring badly. She sat dismal and silent at Matt's side, speaking only when spoken to, and then less than cordially. Once, looking at her dejected expression, Fleur was shocked to find herself feeling sorry again for the woman who had wreaked so much misery in her own life, and it was with relief she greeted Don Esteban's announcement that it was time for the fireworks, a certain indication that the evening was about to come to a close.

With much laughter, the horde of guests trooped onto the lawn of the spacious home to view an astonishing display of multicolored bursts exploding against the velvet sky.

Promptly at eleven Ramon arrived, spoke a few minutes with Matt, and then stood at attention as the four of them thanked Don Esteban for his gracious hospitality.

When they were within sight of the hacienda, Eric turned to the silent Rita and said casually, "You seemed a little out of sorts this evening. Is something amiss?"

"Mind your own bloody business!" she snapped.

A cynical smile spread over his face, but he said nothing more and neither did Matt, seated in front with Ramon. When they reached the front door, Rita was the first one out of the car, appearing in a great hurry to get into the house.

Matt's silky voice stopped her. "You

aren't retiring so early, I hope. I want to speak to you."

"Can't it wait until tomorrow?"

Matt's voice was quite persuasive. "I've been waiting all evening."

What is the matter with the man? Fleur thought angrily. Two hours ago Rita had told him she was ill and now when she was finally home, he was selfishly detaining her. Amazed at her defense of the enemy, Fleur joined Eric and Matt at the doorway, which Rita still blocked.

"I'm very tired," Rita said.

Matt took her arm, and as though oblivious to her drawn appearance, said smoothly, "You look splendid. Surely you have the strength to join me in a nightcap." Ushering her firmly toward the living room, he said to Fleur and Spandell. "You'll excuse us, I'm sure." Then he stepped into the living room and closed the double doors behind him.

"Eager, isn't he," commented Eric sourly. 'And where does that leave you and me?"

"Exactly where I want to be!" snapped Fleur. "On *this* side of the door."

Eric chuckled. "Then as a couple of unwelcome outsiders, shall we find a drink of our own?"

Fleur cared nothing for sharing a drink

with Spandell, but her anger would hold sleep at bay for hours, she knew, so she followed him reluctantly toward the kitchen. She had never set foot inside Josie's domain and hesitated to do so now, certain that when the cook appeared in the morning she would not take lightly to intruders who had disarranged things in her absence.

When Spandell threw open the door, however, Fleur was surprised to see Josie had not yet retired. The kitchen was ablaze with light, and at the table in its center, the ordinarily placid cook was engaged in an animated conversation with Antonia and Ramon. Their chatter ceased abruptly at the appearance of Fleur and Eric.

Wringing her apron nervously, Josie approached. *"Ah, señorita! Señor!* You are hungry, no? I fix!"

"No, no." Eric raised a calming hand. "Only thirsty. Do you have the mixings for a nightcap out here?"

Josie blinked.

"Margaritas perhaps?"

Ramon said something swiftly in Spanish and scurried toward the cabinets. Antonia slumped wearily in her chair, seemingly too exhausted to bestir herself for anyone.

Within minutes Ramon had produced a

pitcher of the icy tequila drink and two glasses on a tray.

"The patio will do nicely," said Eric, and soon he and Fleur were settled beneath a canopy of stars.

"Well, Kirkpatrick was certainly hot to be alone with Pittman, wasn't he?" He spoke bitterly. "It's pretty obvious he doesn't care what we think."

Fleur glanced across at him. The idea returned that Eric might still care in some twisted way for Rita despite his constant deprecating remarks about her. *Had* they spent the night together the evening Ramon's brother was killed? She set down her glass and spoke carefully. "I couldn't care less what they do."

"Really? Just what is the score between you and Matt?"

"That's rather obvious, isn't it? I was careless with the Vera Cruz bowl. He despises me."

"The opposite appeared true on the float."

Fleur's heart lurched, but she managed a cool response. "That was strictly for show."

"Ah. Then the war is still on?"

Fleur saved herself a reply by sipping from her drink. In a moment he went on in a

223

moody tone, "They were thick as thieves while you were in San Cristobal. Kirkpatrick didn't let her out of his sight."

Fleur bit back her anguish. "That must have pleased you." Then aware that perhaps she had been cruel, "You're always so anxious for Rita not to be upset."

"I did relax quite a bit in your absence," he admitted. "That was a smart move of yours, getting yourself out of the way."

Fleur wanted to blurt out that it was not smart at all, only desperate, but she held her tongue.

He went on in a musing tone. "That gift of Don Esteban's this evening. What did you make of that?"

Fleur spoke hesitantly. "I – I wondered if somehow Don Esteban knew that I – that Matt had lost his original Vera Cruz and the presentation was his way of making up for it."

"With an imitation?" Spandell's voice was scornful. "I hardly think so."

He poured himself another margarita and settled back on the bench. The moon, sliding out from behind a cloud, revealed a puzzled look on his ordinarily self-assured face. "But there was something funny about it."

Fleur pulled her mind back from

wondering what might be going on in the living room. "What?"

Spandell's small brown eyes were narrowed. "I don't know what. But Rita did. And it made her sick."

Could he be right? Fleur thought again of Rita's peculiar lack of interest in Matt's attentions. "I think it was probably the excitement, as she said."

Spandell snorted. "Nonsense! She thrives on being the center of attention. At least ordinarily."

Fleur waited.

"If Kirkpatrick blows this deal right here at the finish..." Spandell spoke through tight lips. "I'll have his head!"

"What are you talking about?"

"It was plain Rita didn't care to be alone with him, wasn't it?"

"Well – yes."

Spandell, no longer relaxed, sat coiled on the edge of the bench. "There's something fishy here. And I don't like it. I don't like it one bit."

Fleur stood up, suddenly worn to the bone with anger and disappointment and disillusion. "Well, I for one am not going to waste another moment's thought on any of it. I've done everything I can to hold up my

225

end of the project. If it falls through now, I can't help it."

"I don't believe those are your true feelings." Spandell stood too. "It matters just as much to you as it does to me what's going on in there." He jerked his head toward the living room.

Fleur longed to remind him that another time on a night much like this one she had expressed concerns of her own, and he had callously walked away. "I think you're overreacting. Rita was ill and unresponsive to Matt because of that." But knowing Matt... She swallowed painfully. He'd bring her around soon enough. She had a quick picture of the two of them locked together as they had been in Spandell's photograph. "I'm going to bed," she announced sharply.

"Sleep well," Spandell sighed, "if you can."

Chapter Eighteen

Fleur prepared for bed slowly, finding herself drawn more than once to stare across the patio to the living room where lights still burned, though now the door was half-

226

opened. The patio itself was empty, Spandell having shortly decided he cared less to sit alone in the moonlight than to finish his drink in his own room.

What was going on in the living room all this time? She pressed her cheek against the cool glass. Since the door was open, there could scarcely be anything of a physical nature taking place. Perhaps the room was empty, perhaps both Rita and Matt had gone to bed and simply left the lights burning.

Staring in the direction of the living room, Fleur fought an impulse to put on her robe and go and see for herself. A ridiculous idea, of course. No matter what her pretext, she would appear a fool if, by chance, the conference was still in progress.

Conference. She turned down her mouth wryly. Slim possibility it had ever been that. "Tryst" was a better word. But why in the living room then? Why hadn't Matt chosen some secluded spot to be alone with Rita?

Fleur turned back to the dressing room, and taking up a brush, began to stroke the heavy masses of her dark hair, remembering with pain Matt's strong, blunt fingers threading it as he held her near.

Christmas together in New York. How heavenly that could have been! Could she have so completely misunderstood him that day at Progreso? Had he been handing her a line, never caring in the least whether or not she took him seriously?

Everything indicated that. Except her heart. A flame still flickered there loyally. *A shrine of love,* she thought mockingly.

She turned out the light and crawled between the silken sheets Antonia changed daily. She would miss the luxury of living at the hacienda. Nothing was wanting for their comfort. Matt had seen to that. He was a superb host even if his guests were not entirely welcome. Her throat tightened. Had she ever convinced him of the significance her designs would play in the exhibition? Had he ever really cared when he sat listening so intently, his dark eyes burning into hers? Or had he only been wondering how soon she would be quiet so that he could take her into his arms and gratify whatever feelings he had for her?

What feelings *did* he have?

None, some part of her responded. What had happened this evening was clear enough indication of that. His eagerness to be alone with Rita was plainer than if he had announced from the float in the village square that Rita Pittman was the only woman he cared for.

What a funny little contraption the float had

been, Fleur thought with a sad smile. That rickety old chair gilded so splendidly. Rita's throne. And the hours it must have taken someone to cut and tack all those crepe-paper roses! Suddenly she saw Rita's face again as she had looked when she opened the box, the orange bowl tumbling across her lap

Fleur sat up in bed and stared thoughtfully out at the moonlit patio. There was honest shock in that expression of Rita's. Horror, almost. Why? Did she think, as Fleur had, and Eric too, that somehow Don Esteban had secured for Matt a replacement of the bowl she had broken! Had guilt overwhelmed her at last?

Suddenly Fleur was aware of movement near the fountain in the center of the patio. Tensely she watched while a shadow grew larger on the white stones. Someone was walking in the path of light streaming from the living room.

She lay back quickly, feigning sleep, but with her eyes narrowed toward the glass door. A form stopped just beyond it. Fleur's blood froze. Was it Rita? What did she want? The moonlight intensified, outlining broad, shoulders, a familiar thatch of short, dark hair. Matt!

She lay without breathing. He was facing her room, staring. Then he turned, moving away with a hesitant step in the direction by which he had come.

Fleur's breath escaped her in a rush. What had he wanted? Had Rita told him some new lie to turn him against her? Why had everything gone wrong when all she wanted was to be sheltered in his arms, to hear his heart steady beneath her ear, to know that any instant his tantalizing mouth might slide over hers, sparking desire more explosive than any fireworks display could ever be?

She lay on her side, hot tears passing from her cheeks to the pillow. *Matt, Matt.* Oh, why had she ever come here?

Sometime later Fleur woke, instantly tense. There were footsteps in the hall. Matt again? She sat up, the sheet pulled to the creamy breasts spilling from her nightgown. Would this wretched night never end?

Though she strained with every nerve, she caught no sound beyond the soft padding that had awakened her. Gradually her tension eased. She had been dreaming, reliving, perhaps, Matt's mysterious visit to her patio door.

Chiding herself, she lay down, but was bolt upright again in half a second at the sound of the jeep door slamming, its motor turning over.

Someone *had* been in the hall! And now they were riding off.

Reaching across to the nightstand, she turned on her light. Three thirty. She stared blankly at the tiny watch face. Surely it must be closer to morning than that. Why would anyone be setting out in darkness? Spandell? But he was a notoriously late sleeper. Rita was ill, so it couldn't be she.

Matt, then? But why was he walking in their wing? She felt her blood congeal. Of course. He had come from Rita's room. When he had stood in the patio earlier, he had not been seeking *her,* but Rita in the next room! They had arranged a real tryst, and Matt had bungled the directions.

Snapping out the light, she lay down, rigid in the grip of fury mingled with pain. How she despised this place and everyone in it! Spandell pretended to hate Rita, and yet he was jealous of Matt's relationship with her. And Matt! She clenched her fists beneath the sheet. He moved from one woman to another like some gluttonous bee lording it over a garden. Disgusting! Thank heaven in a few days she'd never have to lay eyes on him again.

But where was he going now, hours before daylight? Maybe Rita was with him. Probably Rita's room was too confining for the magnitude of their romance, and they had gone to seek the wide open spaces!

"Well, let them!" she muttered fiercely. "And may the *garrapatas* devour them!" She struck her pillow a blow and buried her head in the hollow. What she wouldn't give never to have heard of the Yucatán peninsula.

The house was strangely quiet when Fleur woke four hours later, drugged by the heavy sleep she had finally fallen into after the jeep's departure. Sun was streaming through the patio door, but there was an eerie silence beyond it.

Hurriedly she dressed, feeling strangely disoriented, as if the time between the last brushing of her hair and the firm strokes she was applying now had been only an instant, one day running into another. Yet she felt rested, as if she had slept for a week.

The hallway was quiet too. Ordinarily at this hour Antonia would have been dusting the little tables and the ornately carved chairs that lined it. But Antonia, too, had seemed strange last night in the kitchen. And Josie. How nervous *she* was!

Fleur sighed in exasperation. Her own nerves must be terribly frayed that she was reading mystery into everything. She turned toward the dining room, expecting to see her three companions seated at breakfast, but though the table was laid for four, no one had eaten.

Fleur glanced around in bewilderment. Where was everyone?

A quick step sounded behind her, and turning, Fleur saw Matt, newly shaven and rested, standing in the doorway. Apparently a night of love had refreshed him, she thought grimly.

He smiled. "Good morning."

Fleur nodded curtly and took her seat at the table. Before either of them could speak again, Spandell burst through the front door, and casting a quick look into the dining room, called out, "Don't wait for me. I want to spread out these prints on the patio. They're still a little damp."

Matt rang the bell for Josie and took his place at the head of the table. "Did you sleep well?" he asked Fleur.

"Yes, thank you." A lie, but what did it matter?

Josie swung open the kitchen door and placed a platter of eggs and bacon in the center of the table. Fleur raised her face to smile at the cook, of whom she was genuinely fond, but found herself staring instead at the curio cabinet beyond Josie.

On the shelf that had previously held the

Vera Cruz glaze, Don Esteban's orange bowl now occupied the place of honor. Humiliation scalded her cheeks. Matt had placed it there to shame her!

His cool voice broke through her stunned silence. "It looks very nice, doesn't it?"

"Pass the eggs, please," she replied coldly.

"That touch of color brightens the whole room, I think."

It was on the tip of her tongue to answer that even a beautiful bowl was not worth humiliating another human being over, but Spandell entered, talking, his face flushed with hurry.

"Sorry to be late. I got up early thinking I'd be finished in time for breakfast, but a roll of film was missing, and I had to make an extra trip back to the house to see if it was in Rita's bag." He helped himself to eggs and toast. "A lot of good it did me. I couldn't rouse her."

"Small wonder," thought Fleur.

Matt put down his fork. "Rita's gone."

"Without me?" Spandell scowled. "She knows we have to work together today or we'll never be finished in time for the Sunday flight."

Fleur felt a peculiar prickling at the base of her scalp. "What do you mean 'gone'?"

Matt met her gaze. "She's left the project."

Spandell's fork clattered to his plate. "The hell you say? She can't do that!"

"I'm afraid she has nevertheless."

"Why?" Eric's small brown eyes narrowed to viperish slits. "Did you rough her up last night?"

Fleur stared. Not once had Spandell spoken with anything but respect to Matt. Rita must be far more important to him than even she had supposed.

Matt, however, appeared amused rather than offended by the remark. "Rough her up? Hardly. Though we did quarrel."

"No wonder!" Spandell replied hotly. "She told you she was ill, and still you insisted on –"

"On the truth." Matt's voice was calm. "And I got it."

Fleur's pulse quickened. "The truth?"

"About the bowl."

"What are you talking about?" asked Spandell.

Matt regarded him quietly for a moment. "You really don't know, do you?"

"Please!" begged Fleur.

Matt's gaze softened. "I made Rita confess she'd taken the bowl from your room."

Fleur clutched the table's edge. "Thank God!"

"Well, I did know *that,*" muttered Spandell.

"Did you also know," said Matt, "that the fragments she produced with such drama in the living room were not the pieces of the original?"

"What?" cried Spandell and Fleur in chorus.

"Not even Rita could stoop to smashing a true artifact."

Fleur's eyes shot to the curio cabinet. "Then –"

Matt smiled. "That's right. What you see is the original safe and sound."

Fleur slumped limply in her chair, but Spandell bounded up and went to peer through the glass front of the cabinet. "I'm damned if I can tell the difference. This isn't your gift from Don Esteban?"

Matt moved to his side, unlocked the cabinet, and set the bowl before them on the table. "Look at the color tracings," he said. "See how smooth the edges are? That's the result of a process no one has yet been able to duplicate."

"Not even Akumal?" said Spandell, naming the potter whose imitation Don Esteban had presented to Matt.

236

"No one."

Fleur leaned closer and let her eyes feast gratefully on the prize that had caused her so much anguish. "I can't believe it's really all in one piece."

Matt took it up and held it out to her. "Now you can examine it to your heart's content."

Fleur recoiled. "No, thank you! I'll not touch it again, not for any reason!"

Matt laughed. "I trust you."

The words, meant in jest, fell like hammer blows on Fleur's still unhealed wounds. "How you've changed," she said curtly.

Brick red suffused above Matt's collar. He locked the bowl in the cabinet and took his place again at the table.

"Cold eggs anyone?" Spandell's small eyes darted between Matt's grim face and Fleur's pale one.

Matt rang at once for Josie. "I'd like to explain what happened if anyone cares to listen."

"I know what happened," said Spandell. "Or at least enough to put the pieces together." He laughed hollowly at his own joke and helped himself to the hot food Josie brought from the kitchen. "Rita couldn't stand your attentions to Fleur, so she cooked up a scheme to turn you against her." His

237

penetrating gaze settled on Fleur's drawn face. "It worked too. Her schemes always do."

"Only up to a point," replied Matt tersely.

"Well, that's past history," said Spandell. "What matters now is where we go from here. Do we simply throw in the sponge and forget the whole thing?"

"Just because Rita's gone?" snapped Fleur. "Don't be ridiculous."

"What do you suggest then?" Eric eyed her coldly. "Are you capable of coordinating into a prestigious exhibition the work we've done here?" He marshalled his questions like an inquisitor. "Can you formulate a program from four or five hundred photographs and artifacts? *I* certainly can't. So it's you or nothing."

Fleur bit her lip. Spandell had struck straight through to the heart of the problem, and of course she had no answer. Without Rita's expertise all that remained was a conglomeration of unrelated data. And without the exhibition to launch them, what good were Fleur's designs?

A heavy silence settled over the table while Fleur and Eric regarded each other dismally. When Matt's calm voice broke through, they could scarcely believe their ears.

"I'm prepared to take over Rita's place, if you wish."

Eric found his tongue first. "You! But you've despised the whole affair from the start. I should think you'd be delighted at its failure."

"It's true I've felt strong opposition to my stepbrother's plans." Matt looked at Fleur. "I still do. But I've watched how hard you've worked. I'd be subhuman not to avert wasting that work if it were in my power to do so."

"You'd put aside your own feelings to help us?" Fleur stared.

"Wait a minute." Spandell's eyes narrowed. "You'd be a fool to saddle yourself with a headache of these proportions simply out of the kindness of your heart."

Fleur eyed him coldly. "What better reason could there be?"

"There's something in it for him," Eric turned to Matt. "Am I right?"

Matt looked wryly at him. "You expect everyone to play the game as you do, don't you, Spandell?" He sighed. "But as it happens, there *is* something in it for me."

"I knew it!"

"I talked to Flaxendon this morning. In exchange for my seeing the exhibition through to a finish, he's agreed to return the

239

artifacts to the National Museum in Mexico City."

Fleur and Eric gasped. "That's quite a coup," said Eric with obvious admiration. "You really put the screws to him, didn't you?"

"He won't come out too badly," said Matt. "The Mexican curator has agreed to loan the artifacts to Philadelphia once every four years if Flaxendon will send the complete exhibition."

"Why, that's smashing!" cried Eric. "A far better arrangement than the original one. Now instead of all this work being viewed for only three or four months, there'll be a permanent exhibition!" He rubbed his hands in delight. "You've been a busy boy this morning, Dr. Kirkpatrick."

"Thank you," said Fleur quietly. "You've acted very generously. Eric and I are certainly indebted to you."

"My pleasure."

His gaze was full upon her. Fleur looked away. "What will become of Rita now? Will what's happened spoil her career?"

Eric stared in astonishment. "Do you really care if it does?"

"From what I've seen, she has a great deal to offer the archaeological field. It seems a shame for all that knowledge and ability to go to waste."

Eric seemed sobered by her words. "She *is* damned good." His jaw hardened. "But her temperament always interferes, always spoils things."

What things? Fleur wondered. Was he nursing fresh wounds at her unannounced departure? Wounds that had nothing to do with her professionally?

Matt spoke. "I don't think she'll have a great deal of difficulty finding another position. Of course, the fact that she abandoned a project could be a black mark, but frankly, I think she's ill. I suggested counseling or therapy."

Eric sniffed. "I can imagine her reaction to that."

"Surprisingly, she didn't scoff," replied Matt. "I think this time she had exhausted herself as well as everyone else."

Fleur looked quickly at him. Was that his reaction to Rita? Exhaustion? What did he mean?

"I shouldn't think she can simply walk away from that stunt with the bowl," said Eric. "Ill or not."

"Well, I for one don't intend to mention it beyond the three of us," said Matt. "And Don Esteban, of course."

Fleur's brows drew together. "Don Esteban?"

"I knew there was something fishy about that presentation!" said Eric. "You rigged it, didn't you?"

Matt nodded. "It's a long story. I won't go into it now. I'll simply say it forced Rita's hand, and when I got up this morning I discovered she'd gone. Now –" he turned to Fleur "– I'd like you to come with me to Progreso."

"Today?" Fleur stared. "I'm sorry, but I'll be busy today." Did he actually think now that Rita had deserted him, he could take up with Fleur as if nothing had happened?

"I'm afraid I must insist."

"For heaven's sake, Fleur!" Eric scowled. "The man has been generous enough to pull us out of an impossible situation. The least you can do is cooperate."

"I'm not aware of anything further having to do with the project that remains to be explored in Progreso," Fleur replied icily.

"Ah, but you're wrong there." Matt's voice came softly, persuasively. "As the new director, I plan to focus at least one facet of the exhibition on the sea, which had, as you know, a direct bearing on the development of the Mayan culture." He turned a tantalizing smile in her direction. "I should like your ideas on the spot."

"Then Eric should come too," she answered quickly.

"We won't be photographing today," Matt said firmly. "Besides, I'd like for Spandell to get as much of Rita's work in order as he can while we're gone."

"Right." Spandell rose briskly. "I'll get on it right away."

When Eric had gone, Matt turned to Fleur. "Perhaps we can coordinate the shell motif you're using in your designs with a broader display."

Was this really to be a business trip then? If so, she should be feeling relief instead of the leaden disappointment which crowded her heart. "I'll get my sketchbook," she murmured. "I'll only be a minute."

Chapter Nineteen

The main thoroughfare of Progreso was humming with market-day activity when Matt and Fleur turned into it. Across the harbor she could see the fishing fleet far beyond the pier, crowds of seagulls wavering in the cobalt sky above. Her heart ached. Some day she would come back, she promised herself. Some time, years from now, when the pain of losing Matt was less acute, and she could savor without the need to weep the moments of that one lovely day they had shared here.

Matt stopped the truck before the weathered cottage and turned off the motor. "You've said almost nothing." His arm rested just above her shoulders. "What are you thinking?"

Fleur swallowed the lump crowding at her throat. "Well, for a start, I think one display case should contain nothing but shells from Progreso's shores." She turned toward the water so he couldn't see the tears shimmering in her gray eyes. "Then in the next one, we can bring in the same motif with the pyramid designs Eric has photographed and in the artifacts from the cenotes. I have a fabric..."

Her voice died under the gentle pressure of his hand encircling the back of her neck, turning her face to his. "Did you really think I brought you all this way to talk of shells?"

Her voice came out a whisper. "Didn't you?"

In answer, he lowered his face swiftly. His lips covered hers, his arms tightening until her body molded his. He held her fast, exploring the softness of her mouth, kissing her throat, her temples. "Fleur," he murmured against her cheek. "You must know how I feel about you."

Something cold clutched her heart. "Yes, I know." Extricating herself from his embrace, she moved as far away from him on the seat as she could. "You like kissing me. You enjoy my company as long as no one else is available."

"Is that what you really think?" He paled visibly, his eyes glowing more darkly than ever. "You're wrong, you know. I'm in love with you. I have been almost since the first moment I saw you."

A bitter laugh escaped her. "Oh, yes! That's why you were so rude to me at lunch the day I arrived, why you embarrassed me at the table, and scorned my part in the project when we talked beside the pool."

"That's partly why," he agreed. "I don't like the feeling of being enslaved, and that's the effect you had on me. But my feelings for you were also the reason I decided at first to cooperate with the team, to spend so much time working for an exhibition I deplored."

"Rita is the one who persuaded you to change your mind." Anger flashed in Fleur's gray eyes. "Don't pretend otherwise."

"Rita pretended. I let her because it didn't matter to me what she thought." He caught Fleur roughly by the shoulder and pulled her to him. "I only care what *you* think, how *you* feel about me. Admit it, Fleur. You love me too."

"I might have!" she choked. "But you don't want to be loved. You want to be admired, to flit about from one woman to another without a thought of how your flippancy affects anyone else." She struggled free from his clasping arms. "Well, I've had enough, thank you. I'm tired of being dropped twenty stories on my head every time I begin to trust you."

"I *have* disappointed you. I know that."

"And lied to me! Here." She waved toward the sturdy cottage nestled in the sand. "You had a hangover, you said. But you weren't drunk at all! Eric told me the truth."

"I was teasing you that day! You were so annoyed."

Fleur felt tears burning at her eyelids. "Yes! It amuses you to see me angry. Well, you must be enjoying yourself immensely at this moment."

His face sobered. "Not at all. And do you know why? Because I'm scared. I don't know what I'd do if you walked out of my life."

were. I never thought once of th[e]
[w]hen we came back that day, and [I]
[y]ou'd gone . . ." He shook his head. "[I]
[told?] you how alarmed I was."

[I was?] angry," she said stiffly.

[Ange]r is the way I've dealt with
[situati]ons all my life," he said simply.
[When] I met you, I thought it was an
[easy?] way. When I wanted to change, it
[was di]fficult." His eyes pleaded with her.
[Sti]ll difficult."

[She] felt her resistance crumbling, but she
[was si]lent. He went on. "I knew Rita had
[hidden?] the bowl somewhere in the hacienda
[Ev]ery time we went out while you were
[in San] Cristobal, the servants searched. I
[didn't] let Rita out of my sight for fear she
[might] find some way to get it out of the
[house.] I began to be afraid, too, that my
[worr]y for you was showing and that she
[might] possibly topple over the brink of sanity
[and s]mash the thing on impulse."

[But y]ou treasure it beyond all else, don't
[you?]

[H]e shook his head slowly. "Not anymore.
[Y]ou I treasure, but if Rita had broken the
[bowl], that would always stand between us.
[You]'d have your guilt, and I'd have mine.
[I] wanted it restored whole, so our
[relat]ionship could flourish whole." He was

250

"Your fear is well grounded." She
stiffened her spine against the seat. "I'll work
with you until the exhibition is finished, but
I'll never let you touch me again."

"Will you at least listen to what I have to
say?"

"I've heard it all."

He was silent, his brown hands tightening
on the steering wheel. "Do you remember
how you felt that night in the garden when
you tried to explain to me about the bowl,
and I wouldn't listen?"

"Do I remember?" Her voice broke. "Do
you think I can ever forget?"

He turned swiftly toward her. "Then don't
do the same thing to me now. Hear me out,
Fleur. Please!"

Unwillingly, she studied his anxious face.
"Very well. I'll listen. But then I want to go
home. Is that understood?"

Naked relief sent his frown scurrying. "Of
course." He opened the door. "But let's go
into the house. You can be comfortable
there."

The room looking out on the sea was just as
she remembered it. While Matt opened the
windows, Fleur ran one hand gently over the
smooth zapote wood of her chair and let the
serenity of the surroundings permeate her

247

misery. How she loved this house, its spirit, its warmth and contentment.

Matt took a seat across from her. "I want to begin with that night," he said quietly. "That night when you tried to tell me someone had taken the bowl from your room, and I wouldn't listen."

Though Fleur kept her eyes on his face, she said nothing.

"You know how angry I was, so I won't go into that. But –" he leaned forward earnestly "– my anger didn't last even as far as the main road. Believe that!"

"Why didn't you come back then! I was still in the garden." She swallowed. "I was still there when you finally did come back."

"I didn't turn around because the truth dawned on me. It was like a blockbuster, I can tell you, realizing that Rita had broken the bowl, not you. And yet I couldn't fully realize it either. That an archaeologist would do such a thing. No matter how desperate or angry she was, I couldn't believe she'd actually destroy an artifact. And that's when I knew she hadn't."

"What do you mean?"

"I knew she'd broken a fake, and I had a piece of it! In my pocket."

Fleur leaned forward. "The one you picked up from the table!"

"Exactly!"

"You should ha[ ] confronted her there a[ ] he could have saved th[ ]

"I wanted to verif[ ] knew Don Esteban ha[ ] I went at once to Lap[ ] fragment with it. It v[ ] match. Don Esteban con[ ]

"You could at least [ ] told me!"

"I wanted to – and m[ ] way home I realized how[ ] of madness Rita must ha[ ] such a scheme." His e[ ] Fleur's. "I was afraid for yo[ ]

"You could have told[ ] would have kept quiet."

He dropped his forehead[ ] "Perhaps I should have. I do[ ] know I was sure then tha[ ] extremely careful not to ala[ ] way." He looked up to me[ ] again. "That's why I pretend[ ] with you."

"You shut me out. You[ ] without transportation to go[ ] work."

"I was afraid you'd go to Mér[ ] a plane if you had the means.[ ]

248   249

"Your fear is well grounded." She stiffened her spine against the seat. "I'll work with you until the exhibition is finished, but I'll never let you touch me again."

"Will you at least listen to what I have to say?"

"I've heard it all."

He was silent, his brown hands tightening on the steering wheel. "Do you remember how you felt that night in the garden when you tried to explain to me about the bowl, and I wouldn't listen?"

"Do I remember?" Her voice broke. "Do you think I can ever forget?"

He turned swiftly toward her. "Then don't do the same thing to me now. Hear me out, Fleur. Please!"

Unwillingly, she studied his anxious face. "Very well. I'll listen. But then I want to go home. Is that understood?"

Naked relief sent his frown scurrying. "Of course." He opened the door. "But let's go into the house. You can be comfortable there."

The room looking out on the sea was just as she remembered it. While Matt opened the windows, Fleur ran one hand gently over the smooth zapote wood of her chair and let the serenity of the surroundings permeate her

247

misery. How she loved this house, its spirit, its warmth and contentment.

Matt took a seat across from her. "I want to begin with that night," he said quietly. "That night when you tried to tell me someone had taken the bowl from your room, and I wouldn't listen."

Though Fleur kept her eyes on his face, she said nothing.

"You know how angry I was, so I won't go into that. But –" he leaned forward earnestly "– my anger didn't last even as far as the main road. Believe that!"

"Why didn't you come back then! I was still in the garden." She swallowed. "I was still there when you finally did come back."

"I didn't turn around because the truth dawned on me. It was like a blockbuster, I can tell you, realizing that Rita had broken the bowl, not you. And yet I couldn't fully realize it either. That an archaeologist would do such a thing. No matter how desperate or angry she was, I couldn't believe she'd actually destroy an artifact. And that's when I knew she hadn't."

"What do you mean?"

"I knew she'd broken a fake, and I had a piece of it! In my pocket."

Fleur leaned forward. "The one you picked up from the table!"

"Exactly!"

"You should have come back and confronted her there and then!" The anguish he could have saved them!

"I wanted to verify my opinion first. I knew Don Esteban had an Akumal piece, so I went at once to Lapaleta to compare my fragment with it. It was almost a perfect match. Don Esteban confirmed it too."

"You could at least have come back and told me!"

"I wanted to – and meant to. But on the way home I realized how close to the brink of madness Rita must have been to devise such a scheme." His eyes burned into Fleur's. "I was afraid for you."

"You could have told me privately. I would have kept quiet."

He dropped his forehead into his hands. "Perhaps I should have. I don't know. I only know I was sure then that I had to be extremely careful not to alarm Rita in any way." He looked up to meet Fleur's eyes again. "That's why I pretended to be angry with you."

"You shut me out. You even left me without transportation to go on with my work."

"I was afraid you'd go to Mérida and catch a plane if you had the means. I knew how hurt you were. I never thought once of the train. When we came back that day, and I found you'd gone..." He shook his head. "I can't tell you how alarmed I was."

"And angry," she said stiffly.

"Anger is the way I've dealt with frustrations all my life," he said simply. "Until I met you, I thought it was an effective way. When I wanted to change, it was difficult." His eyes pleaded with her. "It's still difficult."

She felt her resistance crumbling, but she kept silent. He went on. "I knew Rita had hidden the bowl somewhere in the hacienda and every time we went out while you were in San Cristobal, the servants searched. I didn't let Rita out of my sight for fear she might find some way to get it out of the house. I began to be afraid, too, that my anxiety for you was showing and that she might possibly topple over the brink of sanity and smash the thing on impulse."

"You treasure it beyond all else, don't you?"

He shook his head slowly. "Not anymore. It's you I treasure, but if Rita had broken the bowl, that would always stand between us. You'd have your guilt, and I'd have mine. I wanted it restored whole, so our relationship could flourish whole." He was quiet for a moment. "Can't it, Fleur?"

"Why did you behave as you did at the fiesta?" she said evasively. "Rita was ill, and you were horrible to her."

"She wasn't ill! When she opened the box and saw the glaze, she knew I was aware of the truth. All she wanted then was to get back to the house and get the bowl before I did."

"Would she have broken it then?"

"Who knows? I hope not, but she might have."

"Did you know where it was by that time?"

"No. That's another reason we had to stay at Don Esteban's. While we were away, Antonia, Josie, and Ramon made their final search. They discovered it in the living room bookshelves just an hour before we were due to return."

Fleur caught her breath sharply. "Do you mean they searched from the time we left at five until ten?" No wonder the three of them were exhausted in the kitchen when she and Eric had gone for a nightcap. And poor Ramon! He had missed the fiesta after all.

Understanding grew. "So that's why you took Rita into the living room when we got home. To confront her with the evidence."

He nodded. "We had a royal quarrel. She

251

tried to blame everything on Spandell. She said it was he who secured the replica from Akumal, that it was his idea in the first place."

"Why would she do that?"

He shrugged. "She hoped she could still salvage something between us, I suppose. Or save face maybe."

"She didn't care for him at all then?"

"In her own way, I suppose she did. He felt the same toward her." He looked at Fleur. "They've been having an off-and-on affair for years, it appears to me."

Fleur nodded reluctantly. "To me too. But he didn't seem especially unhappy this morning when he found she'd gone, only worried about what would happen to his work."

"In my opinion, neither of them is capable of feeling deeply. They're too concerned with their own skins to worry too much about anyone else's."

Fleur's gaze was level. "You cared for Rita."

"No."

"You kissed her at Dzibilchaltun," she said accusingly. "Directly after you left me."

He stared in surprise.

252

"Eric has a picture. And there were other times."

"I won't deny there were. But I never cared for her," he answered vehemently. "I only wanted to make you jealous."

"That's stupid and childish!"

"Of course it is. But it's the way I've always dealt with women – a technique I learned from my father," he added with mild bitterness. "He killed my mother with his philandering. But he got his comeuppance with Mrs. Flaxendon. She led him around by the nose."

"If you despised their behavior so, why did you mimic them?"

"Because until you came, everything seemed so foolish and useless. I distracted myself in any way I could." He looked around the quiet room. "Only here at Progreso have I ever had any peace in Mexico."

"Then this is where you ought to stay."

A light entered his dark eyes. "I intend to. I've decided to give up my half of the hacienda to Flaxendon." Fleur's heart skipped a beat. "You'd actually do that?" Wonder began to swell within her.

"I'm glad to do it." He got up and walked to the window where he stood looking out at the sparkling waves. "It's a relief to be done with quarreling. Soon the relics will be back where they belong. After the exhibition I can put Flaxendon out of mind forever if I release my part of the hacienda to him. Then everything will be straightened out at last." He turned to stare at her. "Except between us." He took in her set face. "Can you ever forgive me, Fleur?"

"I want to," she whispered. "With all my heart I want to."

He came to her swiftly. "Then what's stopping you?"

Tears filled her gray eyes. "Just when I think I understand you, I realize I don't at all. I can't let you go on breaking my heart forever."

He lifted her to him, pressing her head to his chest. "Give us a chance, Fleur."

"I can't forget the way you were with Rita."

"But I wanted to hurt you then."

"What's to keep you from wanting to again?"

"My love for you," he said quietly. "And that makes all the difference. His encircling arms drew her closer. "I'm so new at loving. I didn't know the meaning of the word until I met you." He smiled. "Until you began to preach your little sermons. Now I can't live without it, without you."

She lifted her eyes to his. Could she live without him? "We're from two different worlds, Matt."

"Are we?" He led her to the couch. "In my world there's room now for caring, for sharing. And none for childish games and temper tantrums. There's a place that no one but you will ever fill." His eyes searched hers. "And I believe that in your world there's a place like that for me, too." He lifted her chin. "Tell me true. Isn't there, Fleur?"

Her heart melted. She threw her arms around him and buried her face in his neck. "Oh, yes! Yes, my darling!"

Their lips met, the firmness of his mouth closing over hers, urgently, hungrily, the unyielding tautness of his thighs hard against her own. "Fleur, Fleur." They rocked together, their joy in each other soaring. At last Fleur pulled free, her gray eyes sparkling. "Was that a proposal, just now?"

Laughing, he drew her close again. "You know it was! Was your question an acceptance?"

In answer, she kissed him soundly. Then snuggling close into his arms, she settled deeper into the couch. "Tell me about your life," she said softly. "Paint me a picture."

He laid his head back and closed his eyes.

"There'll be the sound of waves seeking out the shore, and wind, and new shells on the beach at every dawning. There'll be you and me walking on the sand when the sun comes up."

"Will we be married then?"

"We'll be married by the day after tomorrow."

"Day after tromorrow!" She sat up straight, staring.

"Too soon?"

She thought for only a second. "Hardly soon enough!"

They kissed again playfully, joyfully. "But what about Mom and Barb? They'll be disappointed not to be at our wedding."

"Do you think coming to Progreso for Christmas would make up for that?"

"Oh, Matt! Could they?"

"Of course they could – if they will. We'll be in Philadelphia next week. The first chance we get, we'll fly to New York and ask them ourselves." His eyes touched her awe-filled face. "And who could possibly refuse a couple of winners like us?"

She collapsed again upon his chest. "Oh, Matt, my darling Matt." Her voice dropped to a whisper. "Is what's happening really true? Are we really going to be together the rest of our lives?"

"Absolutely?"

A troubled frown creased her brow. "But what about..." She searched for words. "What about my designs?"

He was quiet for a moment, studying her face. "You're worried about your career, your dreams coming to nothing."

Her anxiety grew. "You don't want a career woman for a wife, do you?"

"I want a fulfilled woman for my wife," he answered quietly. "I want a happy woman. I want you." He kissed her lingeringly. "We'll take one thing at a time. The exhibition first. We'll be doing that together. Then we can come back here and talk about the future."

She got up and went to the window. "I'm not sure I could give it up if you asked me to."

"I'll never ask the impossible of you."

"Not intentionally, no." Her throat tightened. "But you can't compromise your own dreams either."

"I see this discussion can't wait as I'd hoped." He came to stand beside her, his arm encircling her waist. "I want you to be all in life that you desire, just as I'm sure you want for me every achievement I'm capable of." He turned her to him. "So there may be times when our work will cause us to go our separate ways briefly, but Progreso will always be home. It's here our hearts will be, and no matter how far we roam, it will draw us back."

She lifted shining eyes to his. "You do love me."

"You *and* yours," he answered, smiling. "My designer wife, and my sister Barbara whom we'll be sending to college, and my mother, who'll never have to worry again about anything."

Fleur's tears spilled over, but when she started to speak, Matt silenced her with a kiss.

"I hope there aren't any rules against providing for one's family," he murmured against her lips. "Because if there are, I've just repealed them. Is that clear, Mrs. Kirkpatrick-to-be?"

"Clear and sweet," she whispered. "Pinch me, please – just to make sure I'm not dreaming."

"My pleasure," he said hoarsely, but the touch of his hands was far from a pinch, and after a moment he enfolded her completely. There was the sound of waves, as he had promised, and of wind, and in her heart, the matching beat of his – strong and true forever.